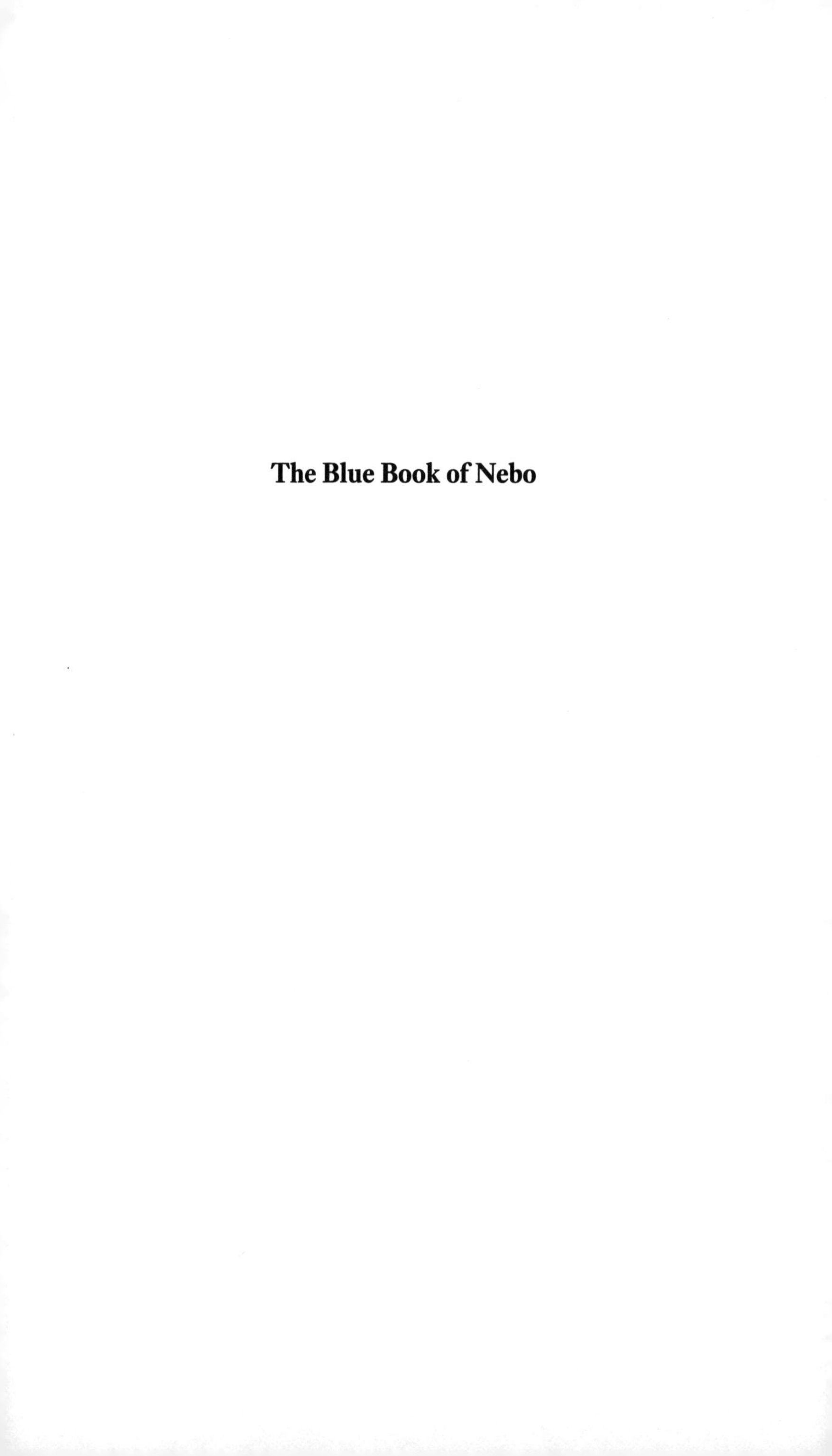

The Blue Book of Nebo

The Blue Book of Nebo

Manon Steffan Ros

Translated from the Welsh by
Manon Steffan Ros

Deep Vellum Publishing
Dallas, Texas

Deep Vellum Publishing
3000 Commerce St., Dallas, Texas 75226
deepvellum.org · @deepvellum

Deep Vellum is a 501c3 nonprofit literary arts organization
founded in 2013 with the mission to bring
the world into conversation through literature.

First edition, 2021

Published with the support of a Wales Literature Exchange translation award through Arts Council of Wales National Lottery Funding.

Support for this publication has been provided in part by a grant from the City of Dallas Office of Arts and Culture's ArtsActivate program.

ISBNs: 978-1-64605-100-7 (paperback) | 978-1-64605-101-4 (ebook)

LIBRARY OF CONGRESS CATALOGING IN PUBLICATION DATA

Names: Steffan Ros, Manon, author, translator.
Title: The blue book of Nebo / Manon Steffan Ros ; translated from the Welsh by Manon Steffan Ros.
Other titles: Llyfr glas Nebo. English
Description: First edition. | Dallas, Texas : Deep Vellum Publishing, 2021.
Identifiers: LCCN 2021008333 (print) | LCCN 2021008334 (ebook) | ISBN 9781646051007 (hardcover) | ISBN 9781646051014 (ebook)
Classification: LCC PB2299.S74 L5813 2021 (print) | LCC PB2299.S74 (ebook) | DDC 891.6/633--dc23
LC record available at https://lccn.loc.gov/2021008333
LC ebook record available at https://lccn.loc.gov/2021008334

Cover design by Marina Drukman | marinadrukman.com

Interior Layout and Typesetting by KGT

PRINTED IN THE UNITED STATES OF AMERICA

To my friend Alun Jones,

who gave me faith in my own voice.

Dylan

Mam says that it's best to write like this now. Because she can't be bothered to teach me, I think, can't be bothered, or can't find the energy. I'm not sure which it is, or if there's any difference.

She used to sit with me for an hour each morning, the hour when Mona sleeps. We did stuff like adding and reading, not like we used to do at school, no graphs or times tables or anything like that. She got me to read books and then I had to write about them, and she marked them with a red biro, telling me where I'd spelled something wrong or said something stupid. And then after doing adding up and taking away, there was no more maths. She started to worry. About the biros too, because we don't want them running out.

'I don't have anything else to teach you, Dylan,' she said yesterday. She'd just read through something I'd written about a romantic novel about a man and a woman who meet on a train, and I think something clicked in her. 'There's no point carrying on like this.'

So she said, as long as I spend an hour writing every day, she wasn't going to bother me with schoolwork anymore.

She got this book from a house we broke into in Nebo. It was in one of the small drawers of a little desk in the corner of someone's living room. Usually, we only steal the really important stuff, like matches or rat poison or books. But she held this notebook in her hands and turned it over a few times before putting it in her bag.

'You have that,' she said later, when we got home. 'To write your story.'

'*The Blue Book of Nebo,*' I smiled, taking the book from her. The pages were blank and wide, like a new day.

'Eh?' asked Mam.

'Like *The Black Book of Carmarthen*, or *The Red Book of Hergest*. That's how they did it in the olden days.' I'd read about them in a book about Welsh history. 'Important books that said something about our history. And now is a part of history, isn't it?'

The book's jacket is a lovely rich dark blue, almost black. *Bible-black*, Dylan Thomas said. But you can tell when a book is a Bible, without even looking at the spine for the title. You just know. My book doesn't look like an important book, but all books are just words strung together.

•

After that, I put the book on the top shelf in case Mona got hold of it, and I went up to the lean-to to fix the corner that's leaking. You wouldn't believe how much water can get through a tiny hole like that. It only needed a tiny lump of Play-Doh and then a piece of tarpaulin on top of that, about two inches square. I could only spare one nail, because there aren't many left. It'll do for now.

Mona started crying, and Mam went to fetch her from the crib.

There's a hell of a view from the lean-to. Down towards Caernarfon, where you can see the castle towers jutting out like gnarling teeth, and then the sea and Anglesey beyond it. I can't ever remember going to Anglesey, but Mam says I went loads of times when I was a little boy. There were nice places to go for walks, Mam says, and loads of lovely beaches all around, because Anglesey is an island. I was thinking about that yesterday when I was sitting on the roof of the lean-to, looking out. Seeing the sea and the island, which looks too big to be an island from here. There are trees and fields and places I don't know between here and the sea. Yesterday was a cold day—cold enough to make my mouth steam, like snow in a saucepan. I sat there thinking about all those people in the olden days, poor things, going to beaches in their cars and sitting there all day with nothing to do. Standing with their feet in the water, then splashing about a bit and then having a picnic. I try not to think about those people too much.

Then I heard Mam coming out with Mona strapped to her breast, and I climbed down the ladder. There was too much to do to waste time thinking about Anglesey and the times that had happened before now.

•

Our house is in a dead place. What I mean is, it's in the middle of nowhere, and no one ever comes here. Well, almost no one. In the olden days, an elderly couple lived in the house called Sunningdale, which is about seventy-eight steps from our house. They went away soon after The End, same as everyone else.

'What's Sunningdale?' I asked Mam one day after I'd been looking though their windows.

'It doesn't mean anything. It's just a word,' she said. I thought meaning something was the whole point of words, but I didn't think Mam would want to talk about that now. Her voice was tired and soft, like a pillow. 'Keep away from that house, Dyl. It isn't ours.'

I think I can remember Mr and Mrs Thorpe, but I can't be sure. He was tall with white hair and glasses that always seemed to be reflecting some light, so you could never quite see his eyes. She was small and thin and stared at you as she spoke. Sunningdale is exactly the same as it was when they left it, except that I've used their garden for planting and I've cut down a few of their trees for firewood. I want to go inside the house, but Mam says no. For some reason, she's a bit funny about Sunningdale and Mr and Mrs Thorpe.

The truth is, they've probably gone forever. They were old, old enough to have stopped working. They did pointless things, like playing golf and growing tiny trees called bonsai in their kitchen window. They could have just gone away to find their families. They might be with them now. Somewhere in England, probably.

Today, I was chopping down branches from their garden to dry out and use as kindling. Mam was standing at the bottom of the tree, and Mona was tied to her chest, trying to talk. Mam was bundling up the branches as I was throwing them down, because that makes it easier to drag them home. It's easier for me to climb trees and to go up on the roof and all that, because Mam has a bad leg and walks with a limp. But she still climbs onto the roof of the lean-to with me when it's sunny or starry.

The curtains have tiny pink flowers on them, and the bed is tightly made, the covers pulled taut and smooth. A wardrobe painted white, and little white tables on each side of the bed, books piled high but tidily on them.

'Come on, Dyl. It's going to start raining properly in a bit!' Mam said, waiting for the branches.

I cut another one and threw it down before saying, 'They've got a lot of books in there.'

Mam was silent.

'And blankets on the bed. A duvet, I think. And two pillows.' I dragged the saw slowly and heavily over another branch.

'It's got nothing to do with us,' said Mam firmly. I knew then that I had to shut up. Mam isn't a woman who argues—she just closes herself, like a door or a book. She thinks that breaking into Sunningdale is different to breaking into the other houses in Nebo, and I can't see why.

She is thirty-six years old today.

We still have the old calendar, the one from 2018, the year The End came. And we can't be certain that we're in the right place, because the days when we were sick at the beginning all went into one mess of time—it might have been three days, it might have been a fortnight. But never mind. We've guessed where we are. Mam doesn't like celebrating, but I think it's a big thing.

Thirty-six years of living! And I've been with her for fourteen of those. She's been with me.

'You've been me with almost half your life,' I said, chucking down another branch.

She stilled and looked up at me through the leaves. Her hair was wet, and she'd zipped up her raincoat over Mona. All I could see of my little sister was a blue fleece hat.

Sometimes I think it's impossible for someone to be as beautiful and ugly as my mother.

I know it's a horrible thing to say. Mam hates it when I call people ugly, even people in stories, and I can't understand that. As long as they don't hear it, what's the harm? But Mam says that the people who see others as ugly on the outside are themselves ugly on the inside. I must be hideous inside because sometimes, I think that Mam is really very ugly.

I don't see many people, so perhaps I can't judge who is ugly and who is beautiful. But I remember The End. I was six, after all, and six years is a long time to collect memories. I think I can remember women looking like they do on book covers—fat pink lips, smooth milky skin, and soft hair with no bits sticking up. Mam isn't like that. She has a long thin face with huge eyes and a small mouth, and a nose that's too long for her face. Her body is tall and strong, not fat but all hard, no soft bits. Before The End, she used to cut it short and dye it blond, but cutting hair is just another job now, and it grows like brambles around her head, thick as dog hair, black as the world goes at night, with tiny silver wires here and there.

I don't think I look like her. I don't look like anyone.

She looked at me for a long time, up in the trees. I thought for a bit that she was going to tell me to break into Mr and Mrs Thorpe's house, but in the end, she just turned away. Mona chatted to herself under Mam's coat—I could hear her voice although I couldn't see her, a disembodied chatter of nonsense words. Sometimes a little hand would reach up to touch Mam's face.

I'll go hunting tonight. Try to get hold of a rabbit or a feral cat so that Mam can have some meat on her birthday. There are traps down on the potato field already. She'll have a good birthday this year.

•

I caught a rabbit yesterday. She was twitching in the trap, so I killed her quickly with my pocketknife and caught the blood in a bottle. Mam makes a sauce with it to put on the potatoes, because it makes us stronger.

She had to drink it sometimes when Mona wanted her milk all the time, because a woman has to be strong to make milk. Sometimes, Mam would drink half a cup of it and throw it all back up again. She says that however cold it is, blood always tastes warm to her, and it makes her feel sick.

I skinned the rabbit and took it home, and said, 'Happy Birthday, Mam.' I'd been to fetch the birthday card this morning and had put it on the mantelpiece. There's a photo of a racing car on it, and 'HAPPY BIRTHDAY—SIX TODAY' written on it, but never mind. That's the only card we had left. I had thirteen birthday cards, but we decided to burn the rest after The End, because we didn't know anything then, not even to store kindling in a dry place for winter.

'Thanks, love,' Mam smiled. Mona was on the floor playing with the toy snake Mam had made out of a sock. I put the rabbit in a pot on the fire.

'Did you skin it?'

'Yeah. Pelt's drying out in the shed.'

Mam nodded.

I don't remember Mam's birthdays before. Well, I remember the most recent ones, of course, but not the ones before The End. But I remember my own birthdays. The cakes and the candles and the shiny wrapping paper on the presents. And I remember the other children's names, though I can't remember their voices or the way they moved or laughed.

Freddie.

Dewi.

Ned.

Ella.

James.

Oliver.

Harry.

Endaf.

Betty.

Swyn.

Eloise.

There must have been more than that, but I can't remember. I've tried and tried, but the more I try, the less I remember. It's like trying to remember a dream.

We ate the rabbit with walnuts. It was lovely. We've kept half for tomorrow, because you'd not believe how much meat you can get off a rabbit.

Tonight, when Mona was in bed, we sat on the roof of the lean-to because it's a clear night.

'You're enjoying the writing,' said Mam, and I wasn't sure whether it was a statement or a question.

'Yeah, but I think something needs to be written

about The End. It doesn't make sense otherwise. And I don't know enough about it.'

Mam nodded. 'You were only little then. It was a long time ago.'

'You should write, Mam. Share the book with me. Just say what happened.'

'I was rubbish at writing at school.'

'You've read thousands of books since then. You'll be better at it now.'

And we agreed, Mam and me, to share *The Blue Book of Nebo*. She'll write about the olden days and The End, and I'll write about now, about how we live. And we've agreed not to read what the other has written, just in case. In case of what, I'm not sure.

'Except if something happens to one of us,' Mam said with a gentle little sigh, and I didn't reply because I didn't need to. I get it. We were quiet for a while.

'I'd love a smoke right now,' said Mam. She says that sometimes in the evenings. Smoking is a thing from the olden days where people put a small thing on fire and then put it in their mouths, then they swallowed the smoke. I can't remember much about it, only the smell. It was warm and thick and lovely to begin with, and then went stale and bitter after a few hours.

'Is that what you'd choose as a birthday present? If you could have anything you wanted?' Mam stared out over Anglesey and thought about it. She smelled like outside.

'Nothing,' she said after a while. 'I wouldn't choose anything.'

That sounded lovely, and I knew it was a lie. Everyone wants something. 'Anything in the world, Mam. Even from the olden days.'

Mam sighed. 'Okay. I'd have a Bounty.'

'What?'

'Bounty. It was a chocolate bar, Dyl.' I can remember chocolate, of course, but not that kind. I remember Dairy Milk and Penguin and Milkybar and Freddo. 'The inside was all pieces of coconut. Sticky with sugar. I always ate the chocolate first, and then the middle bit. The milk chocolate one came in a blue wrapper, and the dark chocolate one had a deep red one.'

'Are coconuts like walnuts?'

'No, no. They're sweet, and they're lots and lots of little bits, all stuck together.'

I regretted asking about it then, because Mam goes quiet when we've talked about the olden days, and it's not the kind of quiet you get when you work but it's a kind of quiet when there aren't any words that fit.

'I never thought about it, you know,' she said after

a while. 'Nobody did. You just walked into a shop or a garage, and if a bar of chocolate or bag of crisps took your fancy, you bought it.' She shakes her head. 'Even if we weren't hungry!'

'But why?'

'I can't remember,' Mam replied. She was quiet for a bit and then she said, 'Because it was there.'

Rowenna

~~I don't know where to start, so maybe it's~~

~~I'm not used to writing. I haven't done for years, since school. But I'm starting to think that~~

~~It's so dark today and it's making me wonder whether~~

I've tried writing things down before, but nothing ever works. It never feels like the truth when I read it back to myself. It feels like it happened to someone else, in a world that was never real. And so many winters have gone by since The End, and I'm scared that if I don't write it now, I never will.

It happened so quickly. The End. I might as well be straight from the very beginning in case you're looking for answers—I don't know what happened. Not properly.

Dylan was in school, and I was at work. I worked in a hairdressing salon, mostly cutting the hair of small children and old ladies. The people between those age ranges tended to go to the more expensive salons in town, where they could get sparkly nails and shaped eyebrows too. I was happy, because I never suited that kind of place or those kinds of people, and Gaynor, who kept the salon, let me finish work in time to pick Dylan up from school. Sometimes, if we were busy, I'd bring him back to the salon with me and he'd sit in one of the leather chairs by the sinks and speak in an old-fashioned way with the old ladies. He knew how to get them to lean over their small boxy bags and unclasp them before offering him a cool pound coin. Gaynor would keep a stash of crisps and Penguin bars in the cupboard under the till, especially for Dyl.

She was kind.

Then, one day, the news came on the radio—we always listened to the radio at work—that bombs had been dropped on some of America's big cities. And Gaynor and I looked up and locked eyes over the heads of our ladies. And after I finished with my customer, I told Gaynor I was feeling unwell, and she gave me the afternoon off. She knew I was lying, but she also knew I wouldn't lie unless I had to.

This is what I did.

Walked to the other end of the village to Mei's Garage, and hired a transit van for the rest of the day. Drove to the big Tesco in Bangor, which was becoming busy with panic buyers like me. And I bought all the dried food I could load into the trolley. Chickpeas and beans, pearl barley, sacks and sacks of different sorts of rice. As many painkillers as I was allowed to, which wasn't that many in case I wanted to kill myself. And then I went on to a huge, cavernous hardware store and bought loads of things I wasn't sure I'd ever need—nails and screws, batteries, two wind-up flashlights, huge sheets of plastic. Two polytunnels—large stiff arches and thick clear plastic sheeting, kind of worm-shaped. Whole boxes of seed packets. Two apple trees (it was spring). A gardening fork and a spade. Rat poison.

On the way home, I stopped at the Spar to get Dylan a couple of Freddos.

Dyma beth wnes i.

I went home and unloaded everything into the garage. Went into the house, and printed page after page of information from the internet. How to make a rabbit trap. How to grow vegetables. Old-fashioned remedies that you could grow in the garden. Which wild plants are safe to eat. How to work out if the water you're drinking is pure.

I returned to the village and took the van back to

the garage, and fetched Dylan. I went to the Spar again to get more chocolate. People had cleared the place of all the tinned food, but there were a few pizzas going out of date, so I bought those for our tea.

Back in the salon, as Dylan was busy scoffing down his Freddos and chatting to an old woman about his teacher, I said to Gaynor, 'You can come and live with us.'

She smiled, a tight little smile I'd never seen before. 'Good God, Rowenna, don't overreact. We'll be fine!' She was brushing the floor, a horizon of gray hairs stretching over the lino.

'Of course we will. But if you ever need to. Come to us.'

Gaynor cleared her throat, as if she was trying to rid her mouth of the words that were threatening to escape. And she carried on cleaning, and we had a coffee, and the hair salon felt like the safest place in the world.

I can't remember what we said after that, but I do remember that before Dylan and I left, she said, 'You've been very good with me.' And I didn't understand, because she'd always been the one who looked after me, just by being in the same place and being the same way every single day I'd known her.

•

Everything was normal for a day or two. Dylan still went to school and I still cut women's hair, and the stack of stuff in my garage started to feel like a foolish indulgence which I'd gone into debt to buy.

Then one morning, as I was painting a pale color into an old lady's hair, the electricity cut out. Just like that. It didn't flicker, just turned off and didn't come back. The radio became silent, and the lady sitting under the lamps murmured, *bloody hell, what now?*

We waited a few minutes, but it didn't come back. I had to rinse the lady's hair with cold water, which she moaned about since she'd only just shaken a cold.

'Is it okay if I pop over to the school, in case they've lost their power too?' I asked Gaynor.

'You might as well go home for the day,' she replied. 'I'll have to close if we don't have power.'

The schoolchildren were playing outside, and I stood there for a bit, watching Dylan. He was pretending to be a plane, two of his friends beside him doing the same. His arms outstretched like a man crucified.

We went home.

The electricity never came back. I waited for it for the first few days, but after a while I seemed to stop hoping. Dylan asked when he'd be going back to school, and I told him that I wasn't sure.

I think I'm hard now.

Sometimes, I think about who I was before. Rowenna, pretty and tidy and always, always, making an effort. The makeup and straighteners and nail polish. Having been on a diet since I was twelve, I am now thin, and muscled, and tired and worried and stern. I haven't work makeup for eight years, and my hair is turning white. I am thirty-six years old.

Dylan

That was a bad day.

Mam had set the trap by the drive next to Mr and Mrs Thorpe's house, and I went out first thing to see if anything had been caught. Today is a blank, browny gray kind of day, but it's bright too, like a dirty blanket. I felt as if the whole world was suffocating—that thick hot air that promises heavy rain. The vegetables need rain, but I need sun.

I hurried over to Mr and Mrs Thorpe's drive, expecting to see the trap empty as usual. It's not the best place to catch anything—the big trap at the top of the lane is far better—but anyway. There was something in the small trap today.

As I got closer, I could see it was a hare, because there was something like brown in his fur, and you don't get that with a rabbit. And it was large, like a cat. It must have heard me coming because it started jumping around, his back paw stuck in the trap.

I don't like killing things.

Mam says that she doesn't either, but that we have to because we need the meat. But she doesn't really mind, I can tell by the look on her face. It's smooth and hard as slate. Like there's nothing warm in her at all.

I don't like the way the knife goes in. The feeling. The sound, too, although I'm not sure if the sound is real or in my head. I don't know whether I could hear the sound of a knife in flesh over an animal squealing. They don't squeal every time, but it's worse when they don't.

They all look at me as they die.

So I walked over to the animal, the lightweight knife heavy in my hand. And that's when I saw.

He wasn't right.

It was a hare, but it was almost two hares. Something was stuck to its head. A sort of lump, and the lump had a small mouth and teeth and two tiny ears. And two dead eyes, as if someone had stolen its eyeballs.

I threw up.

It was disgusting, this two-faced hare, one and a half animals in one creature. And everything that's pretty about a hare was horrible in the second flat, dead face on the back of its head.

The hare was crying.

I don't know what made me do it. I couldn't kill it, maybe because I couldn't ever eat something so awful.

But I could have let it go. But I couldn't do that either. I don't know why.

I went to Mr and Mrs Thorpe's shed, that smells like paint and wood. It's still the same as it was years ago, except that I'd borrowed some old tools and the scythe. Mam made me say 'borrow,' even though I knew we'd never have to give them back.

There was an old white canvas there, all streaked with paint. I took it over to the trap and kneeled down by the hare. It opened its mouth as if it was squealing, but no sound came out.

I threw the blanket over the hare, leaving its head and leg exposed. It was still. I used a stick to prize open the teeth of the trap, and I gently pulled out the hare's leg.

It didn't run away. I lifted it in its blanket and carried it over to the shed. It didn't feel different from any other hare, except that it was shivering. You wouldn't have been able to tell it had a second face, just by carrying it like that.

After leaving it in the shed, I went out and collected nice, soft things—grass and leaves and that sort of thing—so that it could make a little nest if it wanted to. It was hiding behind one of the cupboards. I waited for a bit to see if it would come out, but it didn't, so I left and shut the door behind me.

'Did you get anything?' asked Mam when I went into the house. She'd been collecting nettles for lunch and she was still wearing the gloves.

'It wasn't right,' I replied. Mam stilled and looked at me. 'It had two faces.'

'What?'

'It didn't have front paws. It had another face instead. A dead one.'

Mam looked down again, and gave a long thin sigh. 'Was it hurt?'

'Not much. I let it go.'

Mam nodded. I don't know why I didn't just tell her the truth about the hare in the shed. I don't think she would have understood.

'Bloody Wylfa,' she said then. That's what she said when she saw the baby fox without hind legs, and that squirrel that looked as though half of its skull was missing. I don't know what it means, bloody Wylfa, because it's not in any of the books, and it never feels like the right time to ask.

Dylan

I haven't written for a long time because I don't have a lot to say, but I've got something now.

I've read the book before. It's called *GCSE Biology,* and there's a picture of a skeleton on the cover. Sometimes you can read things and not understand them, or you think you understand them, but when you get older, they mean something different to what you thought. And that's what happened today.

We'd spent the morning fixing the traps in the field, and then Mam said she was going to have a nap with Mona and that I should read or write. So I opened the book at Unit 5, page 62—reproduction.

I had read and had half understood the words before. About the sperm swimming to the egg and then implanting in the lining of the womb, and a little baby growing and growing until it got too big and had to come out. But I'd never put two and two together, because I know that only men have sperm, and that you need sperm to make a baby, but I never thought about what that meant with Mona.

I read it again, in case I'd misunderstood. But I hadn't. And it makes sense too, when you think of the books like *The Color Purple*, and the story of Saint David, the patron saint of Wales, when a bad man called Sant rapes Non to make Dewi. Women have babies after being with a man.

But Mam hasn't seen a man in years. So I don't know where Mona came from.

Dylan

I've been thinking since last time I wrote. Thinking about all the things I don't know.

I don't know why the books talk about a different world, and why some of the animals are odd. I don't know why the people in the books talk to each other all the time, and have lovers, and go out, but that Mam and Mona and me stay here and only see each other. And I don't know how to ask Mam when her face is always like a stone, and her words so few and far between.

Pwyll is getting tame.

I've named the hare with two faces Pwyll. I got the name from an old book, one of Mam's school books—her name is scribbled in the front, Rowenna Williams, year 11. It's a difficult book called *The Mabinogion*, and lots of weird stuff happens in it, and I don't like the characters I'm supposed to like in the story. Heroes are always so sure about what they're doing. But I don't mind Pwyll too much. He makes so many mistakes, but someone still wrote a story about him.

It's a funny name to speak, Pwyll, because it's Welsh and has that weird *ll* sound, like air escaping from the sides of the tongue. It's a whole other letter, and it's hard to say if you're not used to it. I just about remember it from when I spoke Welsh at school, but sometimes I'm afraid of forgetting it, so I say it over and over whilst I'm weeding or making a fire. *ll ll ll.*

Pwyll is a good name for a hare, I think. That *ll* is different but still pretty, an unexpected sort of pretty, just like the hare.

Mam doesn't like writing—she says that everything she writes sounds awkward, not like they do in books, and that I'm good because I put dialogue in and that kind of thing, and that I write how we really speak.

I don't know if I do really, because we don't speak all that much. Mam uses language sparingly, as if it were food. I speak to Mona more than I do with her, and she doesn't know how to reply. But I say things anyway, and she babbles back. I don't know how Mam can stand to be so silent.

It's hard to talk for a long time without anyone to talk back to you. At least I have the books to give me words. I wonder if I talk the same as I would before The End, because sometimes I'll say a word or a sentence and Mam will give me a look. But how am I supposed to know what to say?

'People write differently to how they talk. That's why no one likes writing.'

I wanted to say, which people? And I wanted to ask, are you talking about before The End now, Mam? But I didn't. Because sometimes I catch her looking at this book, at the bit on the shelf where we keep *The Blue Book of Nebo*. I think she has a lot to say, many things she needs to write.

Rowenna

I need to write about Gaynor.

The smell of the salon trailed her like a ghost. Peroxide and almond shampoo and that other smell, damp hair swept to lines on the lino. I never liked the smell of our house when I was a girl, but the scent of Silver Scissors salon was warm and comforting, like some kind of home.

There is so much to say about Gaynor, and about what she meant to her people.

She somehow knew when to chatter and when to stay silent when one of her ladies settled in the chair. Sometimes, people needed to hear endless empty talk about the price of carrots, and the infuriating din of the bin lorry in the morning, and all the shops that were shutting over on the high street in Caernarfon, and how sad it was to see so many empty windows. And sometimes, not often, but more often than you would have thought, she left the air empty, quiet, so that the lady in the chair could let her heavy words fill the silence.

My sister died yesterday.

or

I haven't spoken to anyone in a fortnight.

or sometimes, just tears—silent ones, slipping like yesterday into creased faces.

She began and ended each haircut in the same way—her hands on their shoulders, catching their eye in the mirror. Gaynor had the kindness you always hoped for in a doctor, but rarely got.

'You're very kind,' I said once. 'Helping everyone.'

Gaynor smiled, surprised. I think that kindness was her nature, hers being the only human touch most of the old ladies had in a world that rendered them invisible.

A few years ago, Dylan asked me, 'Was Gaynor my grandmother?' And I blushed for some reason, and replied haughtily, although it was a perfectly reasonable question.

'Of course not!'

'Who were my grandparents then? I can't remember them.'

I swallowed and swallowed and swallowed, even though I didn't cry much by that point because I'd already started to become hard. 'Gaynor wouldn't mind if you thought of her as your grandmother, so you can if you want to.'

Blood is thicker than water, but there's so much water.

•

Today it's raining, fat hot raindrops that spit spitefully on the house. And I thought, I'd better write about the water, because there's so much more since The End.

Rain isn't the same as it was. It's not the kind of rain I stood in by the school gates waiting for Dylan, nor the sort of lazy gray drizzle that made us want to snuggle up on the sofa and watch a film. It's angry now. Not just the rain—all of the Weather.

That's another thing, since The End. Without other people, and without the radio and Snapchat and Facebook, I see human emotions everywhere. The potato field is kind on a warm spring day. The house is fed up and has allowed another hole in the roof. And the Weather, always, a temperamental and untrustworthy lover that I can't break free from, a man that loses his temper over nothing.

I always think of it that way—Weather, with a capital W, the devil by my door. It's cruel in the winter, sulky and frozen, thick, soft snow barricading us in the house. But the summer is so much worse. That's when its heat is oppressive, killing plants and gulping all the water with its vindictive cruelty.

The worst thing is not knowing whether the weather really is any worse, or if I'm only noticing because I depend on it to grow food.

The rain, the hot, violent, ugly storms. Blades of lightning, sometimes with no warning, poking the earth as if checking to make sure it's dead. The thunder like something massive breaking, and the rain creating new rivers. Dyl and I sit on the lean-to in our raincoats, naming them. *Fern River, Dirt River, Sunningdale River.*

Fear is a different thing since The End. It's softer, because it never leaves, and it's not as powerful as it used to be. I used to worry about paying the insurance and that my jeans were too tight, and that I looked old. Now I worry about the potato harvest, and about someone coming here, maybe, and killing us all. And I worry about the nothingness that is everywhere. All signs of life are gone—no lights, no smoke. Sometimes, Dylan and I walk the fifteen minutes across the fields to the lake in Cwm Dulyn to swim and wash, and there, more than anywhere, I feel like we're the only ones left, trying to survive in the mountains, alone.

'It's like Noah's flood,' said Dylan last night, as one of the first storms of spring tried to break into the house. My son, who has never stepped foot inside a chapel or church, who was conceived in a hot tangle of unforgivable sins, knows his Bible. He says he likes the stories. Especially the one about Noah, where God gets rid of everyone and everything in order to start again.

Dylan

She doesn't say anything, but I don't think Mam likes that I read the Bible.

We only had a copy of the Bible, a big, heavy slab of a book with tiny writing and pages like tissue. But then I found a small copy of the New Testament in a handbag hanging on someone's dining room chair in Nebo, and I thought how odd it was that someone carried that around with them, with their purse and sunglasses and phone. It fits perfectly into the back pocket of my jeans, and it's really old.

Inside, someone has written, *To Trevor Evans, for the best design of a Xmas card. Rector. Llanbrynmair. Xmas 1925* in tidy, rounded handwriting that leans to one side.

I like the story.

There are stories that don't really make sense to me—stories about the years before The End, stories about games and phones and cars and computers. I follow the stories, but they don't make sense to me in the same way as they would have if the world was still the same as it was back then. They write about those things as if they're natural and normal. And even though the stuff in the Bible happened a long, long time ago, they make sense in our world now. It feels like Jesus Christ is talking about Mam and me, and only us, when he tells God before he's crucified, *I pray for them: I pray not for the world, but for those whom thou hast given me; for they are thine.* (John 17:9) There's not much point in praying for the world, but me and Mam may just have a chance.

A funny thing:

When I was at school and we had to sing songs in assembly and pray at the end of the day and speak Welsh, they told us about Jesus Christ and the Bible and some of the stories in it. They made him sound a bit wet and pathetic, the kind of man who always has sad eyes. But once, when they asked us to draw a picture of Jesus, one of the kids did a huge color drawing of a big black man with a massive smile and normal, colorful clothes. And everyone went, *That's not what Jesus Christ looked like!* But by then, he was in my head that way, and that what he's still like.

In school, they called him his Welsh name, Iesu Grist. And even though I read the Bible in English, I always think of him as Iesu, not Jesus. Jesus sounds like a weak goody-goody. Iesu sounds like a man.

I think of the stories as I work, and I think about

how Iesu was kind and nice and loved everyone, but he still lost it sometimes. And the way the gospels all tell the same story but someone different tells the story each time, because every story looks a bit different depending on who you are. Sometimes, that makes me think about this little book, *The Blue Book of Nebo*, because Mam and me are probably telling our truths in different ways.

I've promised not to read what Mam writes.

One of my favorite things about Iesu is the way he doubted God at the very end. When he was on the cross, he said, *My God, My God, why hast Thou forsaken Me?* (Matthew 27:46) Because doubting and losing faith means that Iesu was a normal man, even though he did miracles and that.

Sometimes, I tell Mona some stories from the Bible. She comes with me often if I go into the polytunnel or out to collect nettles or to weed out the potatoes. When she was little, I tied her to my chest with the sling, but now I tie it in a different way and carry her on my back instead. I like the feeling of her there, warm on my spine as I work, and I'm always chatting away to her, even though she's only just started putting words together.

I was walking up to the lake in Cwm Dulyn with her yesterday, because it was sunny and I thought we should wash. Mam was washing clothes in the stream, so I put Mona on my back, and off we went.

'Dyl sing,' she said as we crossed the potato field, so I sang for her. Silly songs from my head to start off with, and then a song about Noah's ark, and then a Welsh song called "Mae Iesu'n Ffrind i Mi," which means "Iesu Is Our Friend" (but I couldn't remember any more words than that.) She fell asleep on my back, her hot breath tickling my neck. I could feel her even though I couldn't see her.

After we washed and dried and walked home, the three of us sat in the garden to eat our supper, and everything was pretty and perfect and somehow hopeful. Our clothes were bright and clean on the line, and Mam was in her shorts and had loads of little brownish freckles on her legs, and Mona was chattering to herself as she shoved leaves and grass into the little den I'd made for her under the hedge. *Maaaam and Dyyyyl and Moooooona and Maaaaam.*

'D'you remember pizza?' asked Mam suddenly. She was lying on the grass, her long plait like a snake in the grass. An asp.

'Yeah. Not very well.'

'D'you know what?' She sat up. 'In the cities, even in the ones close to here, like Bangor, you could phone up and get someone to come out to your house with a pizza.'

'Eh?'

'You told them what you wanted on it—say pepperoni and ham—and then they cooked it, put it in a box, and brought it to your house.'

'But why did anyone need to do that? Didn't they have an oven?'

'Yeah, everyone had an oven. Just that sometimes, people couldn't be bothered to cook.'

That's weird to me. Because cooking is a lovely thing. You make something, and then you get to eat it.

Sometimes we have these chats, sitting out in the garden or on the lean-to at night, or in front of the fire when it's snowing outside and we're trying not to worry that the vegetables won't freeze in the ground and die. Chats about what it was like before The End, things like the internet, which was massive and full of knowledge and pictures and words, but no one knew where it really was. Or wars, when important people argued and then got less important people to kill one another. Mam says, *It made sense before The End* a lot, but I think that what she actually means is that it doesn't make sense anymore, and maybe those two things are slightly different.

Sometimes I want to ask her other things about before The End. Things about me and how I came to be and who am I like? Who do I resemble? But I don't ask, because Mam only ever tells me what she wants to tell. I have to guess a lot.

'Imagine if we could call for a pizza now,' I said. I can't remember the taste of pizza, but I like the sound of the word, which is sunny and warm. 'And someone brought it here in a box.'

Mam shook her head. 'I wouldn't do it. I wouldn't go back to living like that.' She smiled at me then, a huge smile that made her look too young to be my mother. 'We're doing okay, aren't we?'

I nodded. 'Yeah. We're okay.'

We both looked over at Mona, who was singing a silly song I'd made up for her. *Noah's a-a-ark, Noah's a-a-ark, it's raining, it's raining* . . . And she threw the leaves up so that they fell like rain on her head. Mam laughed.

'We're okay. But I'd give up this house and everything in it for a sausage roll right now.' We both smiled. Then we lay in the grass until the first stars came to pierce the sky.

Rowenna

I haven't explained about the books.

This was in the early days, after the electricity went off but before the cloud came. The End was a process, not one moment. And this was at the beginning of The End.

I decided to go down to the village to see what was happening. The electricity had been off for about a week, and Dylan and I had done nothing much, as if it was a school holiday, just pottered around the house, put up the first polytunnel, a few chats with Mr and Mrs Thorpe next door.

We were in the garden with Mr Thorpe when he said, 'You could pop down to the village, you know. Susan and I could watch Dylan. Or . . . if you need to go and pick someone up, bring them here . . .'

I stared at him, not quite comprehending.

'Family, maybe?'

I shook my head firmly. 'No family.'

'No parents?' Mr Thorpe asked quietly, thinking, perhaps, about his own sons.

(There are some things that should be noted in *The Blue Book of Nebo*. Other things should not.)

'No parents. I'm nobody's daughter.'

Mr Thorpe nodded, and said, 'Well then, if it's just down to the village to see what's happening . . .'

A week before, I wouldn't have considered doing such a thing. Leaving my little boy with two old people who were virtual strangers.

'We'd just play in the garden. I could show him my shed. And, if you would . . . If there's any food for sale down there. We'd pay you, of course.'

But the windows of Spar were all smashed in, and the shelves were empty. It was the same in The Lion, and the Indian. And in Scissors. There were no cars on the road, and I didn't see a single person as I drove through the village. It was as if everything had ended, and leaving a noisy, awful silence on the streets.

I stepped through the front door of Scissors, the glass crunching like sugar under my feet. The till was gone, of course, but someone had gone to the trouble of smashing the mirrors, tearing the wadding from the chairs, overturning the shampoo and conditioner bottles and smearing them on the walls, smashing the sinks. Someone had emptied the bin, too, leaving gray and white curls in little clouds on the lino.

'Gaynor?' I called out, my voice loud and impudent

in the silence of the village. There was no reply. The door that led up to her flat was locked, and no footsteps could be heard either. She had gone.

When I turned to leave, a man was standing in the door of the shop, a black hood over his head and a golf club in his hands. I was too stunned to scream.

'Rowenna? Is that you?' He slipped off his hood, and I sighed, my heart in my throat.

'Bloody hell, Rhys! You nearly gave me a heart attack!'

'Sorry. Sorry, Row.' Rhys set down the golf club. 'I thought it was you—I was watching through my attic window.'

Rhys, who had been in the same science and maths classes as me at school—a set 3 hard man, a beast on the rugby pitch, and a kitten with the girls on a Saturday night. He had been around from the very beginning, one of the lads, but I'd never had a proper conversation with him. Sometimes, you know people without having to know anything about them. They're just there, like the mountain.

'Where is everyone? Where's Gaynor?' I asked.

He shook his head, and I could see the little boy in him, lost and confused.

'Gone. Everyone's gone, more or less. They went to town to look for food, or to find their friends and family or whatever. I was gonna go too, but then I noticed that they never seemed to come back.' He ran his fingers through his greasy hair. He'd always been so handsome and vain before all this. 'But there are gangs, smashing up everywhere looking for cash and food. They've cleaned out the pharmacy.'

'Just because the electric went off?' I asked. And Rhys stared at me over the shop floor, the whole story in his head trying to settle into the correct words.

'I heard on the radio that there was a bomb in London. It hasn't picked up on anything since then. But they say that another bomb has gone off, closer to us . . . Manchester or Liverpool, I'm not sure.'

'Here? Not here! Why would they, there's nothing here!?'

'There isn't now.' Rhys wiped his brow with the back of his hand and suddenly I remembered that he used to do that at school—it was a gesture that was uniquely his. A nervous tic, although I wouldn't have interpreted it that way at school. 'Nuclear, Row. We're fucked.'

A mushroom cloud rose up in my head. I pushed it away to make space for the kind, calming thoughts of reason. *Everything will be all right. They've always been all right before.*

'A nuclear war?'

'I don't know. I don't even know who did it, or why.' Rhys shook his head. 'We've done so many bad things to so many people, haven't we. Britain, I mean.'

'What are we supposed to do?' My voice was bound tight by panic. 'I've got a little boy!'

'Go away. Get away from here. You live in the middle of nowhere, don't you?' I nodded. 'Go back there, and stay there. Lock the door.'

'But Gaynor . . .'

'Jesus Christ, Row! She's gone! This is it!' Rhys looked furious. 'This is The End!'

I nodded slowly, though I didn't understand or accept it. Someone would sort this, surely. The government or the army or.

'Thanks, Rhys.' I stepped past him, without a smile or a hug. I didn't say goodbye to him, or wish him well. But I did steal his word, The End. It was such a dramatic word to come out of the mouth of the laid-back school hunk, and I liked it. The End, and we were still here.

I think that's when I started to become hard.

I probably should have driven home straightaway, maybe, but as I was going towards home in the car, I stopped outside the library. I still don't know why I did it. The windows, at least, were still intact, but the doors had been torn off their hinges.

I stepped into the library.

Someone had taken the gardening books, and the self-help books—also, for some reason, the biographies.

I took what I could. Armfuls of novels, a few travel books, some classics. And the Welsh-language books.

I stood there for a few seconds before taking those, facing that shelf as if I'd come face-to-face with an old enemy.

But I took them, as many books as I could carry in the back seat of my car. I drove home with the smell of paper distracting me from my anxiety, the weight of the words like a family in my back seat.

Mr and Mrs Thorpe nodded when I told them what Rhys had said, as if they'd suspected this all along. They turned to one another and smiled sadly. Mr Thorpe laid a heavy hand on his wife's shoulder.

'Well, that's that,' he said quietly.

They had two sons, somewhere in the south of England—one in London, I think. I used to see them, before The End, coming to see their parents in the summer, and I'd spy on them, a snob in reverse, judging them for their posh accents, their children's Boden clothes, their gleaming, ugly 4x4s.

Mr and Mrs Thorpe didn't see expensive clothes and showy cars in that second of an old man's hand on his wife's shoulder. They saw their babies, the milky smell and soft skin. They saw first steps and tricycles and laughter. And something terrible exploded, silent and still, between them.

I remember those seconds of nothing but breathing between Mr and Mrs Thorpe, a touch, stillness. And nothing was more beautiful than the backdrop—my garden and the trees, Caernarfon and Anglesey on the horizon, and Cwm Dulyn like a womb on the other side. Everything looked as it should, the spring kind and warm around us. It was difficult to believe that bombs could fall from such a brilliant blue sky.

They didn't cry, David and Susan Thorpe—not in front of us, anyway. Susan sank to the grass with Dylan, and they went back to the Matchbox cars that were battling through the dandelion jungle of our garden. David came back to my car to help me carry the books into the house.

'I don't know why I brought the Welsh books,' I

said, just saying something to fill the silence. 'I don't read a lot, to be honest.'

David kneeled and placed the books in a pile in the living room: Thomas Hardy; Jodi Picoult; Dewi Prysor. He stayed there for a moment, pushing his glasses back along his nose. I thought for a moment that he was going to cry, but then he said, 'I suppose instinct makes you save that which you're most in danger of losing.'

(That night, I wrote those words on the back of an old receipt and stuck it on to the fridge with a flower-shaped magnet. *I suppose instinct makes you save that which you're most in danger of losing. David Thorpe, May 2018*)

'What? The books?' I asked.

'The language,' David replied.

'I . . .' I fished around for the words I'd never had to say before. The words people never asked of me. 'I don't speak Welsh.'

'Oh! Really? Didn't you go to school here?'

'Well, yes, but . . . I *can* speak Welsh . . . I'd just rather not.'

'Right,' said David, as if there was so much more he'd like to tell me.

'It's complicated. We spoke Welsh at home, when I was growing up.'

'Goodness. And yet you don't speak it with Dylan.' He smiled sadly. 'Your mother tongue.'

•

They had to be read, of course—novels, to begin with, with a dictionary by my side as I battled through the sentences. There weren't many children's books in the house, and so I started reading the novels out loud to Dylan in the evenings, my tongue tripping over the words and his mind tripping over stories that were too old and complicated for him. But he soon grew. He was reading my GCSE Welsh textbook by the time he was ten and memorized the first few chapters of a few favored tomes. By the time he would have started secondary school, Dylan was reading everything in the house, and was entirely self-sufficient. He knew so much more than the school would have taught him.

And me, too. The stupid, invisible bottom-set girl, the one who gradually dropped her Welsh because all the cool things, the American bands and the English soaps, were in another language. Mrs Ellis, the Welsh teacher, had written in my report, *Her Welsh grammar is lacking, and she often litters her sentences with English.* But that was our Welsh—littered with English, and colloquial and incorrect and perfectly imperfect. She wanted book-Welsh, and I only had my lived-in street-Welsh. I've read all the books now, and I know how to write formal, proper Welsh. I know the work of T. H.

Parry-Williams and Kate Roberts and Ceiriog. I don't know where Mrs Ellis is now—dead, I imagine—but I still get angry at her for her failings. If The End hadn't happened, I'd feel that these books weren't for me, that I wasn't good enough for my own mother tongue. There are so many words I wouldn't have learned if the world hadn't ended.

There's a list on the wall above the chimney breast, a list of new Welsh words for me and Dylan. We don't add to it anymore, but sometimes I look at it, the words that were given to us after the lights went out, and I think of what Mr Thorpe said. Sometimes, I say the words out loud, and it sounds like the Shipping Forecast that used to be on the radio late at night, telling me about all the faraway Weather.

Adwaen means recognize.
Digofaint means wrath.
Einioes means lifetime.

Dylan

At the very beginning, we only had one big polytunnel, and that it wasn't half as good as it is now. It used to flap in the wind and the poles used to fall over sometimes. It leaked air.

Even though I was only six when The End came, I knew almost straighaway what I was good at. After we built the polytunnel and made raised beds with old wooden planks, Mam and I planted the seeds and hoped for the best. But I was the one that watered them. I was the one who separated the tiny seedlings when they needed more space to grow. When it was time, I was the one who collected the seeds ready for next year's sowing.

I remember the first success.

It was after the electricity went off, but before the cloud. It hadn't been long since I'd planted them, but I still raced out to the polytunnel every morning to see if there was anything to be seen in the claggy soil. Mr Thorpe and I had painted small slabs of slate with the names of the plants so that we could remember what was what. For some reason, he wanted to write both the Welsh and the English names, so I had to go into the house to fetch a thick dictionary. Those slates are still there, with Mr Thorpe's slanted handwriting on each one: Nionod / Onions; Moron / Carrots; Rhosmari / Rosemary.

Then one morning, after weeks of watering and watching and hoping, something was there. A tiny, tiny curl of life daring to exist, a flash of green light, a speck in the square of dead soil.

The start of something.

I felt the thrill of it filling my whole body, a new electricity—pride and joy and the miracle that I, somehow, had been a part of creating. This wonderful, tiny thing. I raced upstairs to Mam and shook her awake. 'Mam! It's happened!'

She sat up straightaway, not giving herself time to wake up properly. 'What?' she asked, as if I'd said something terrible.

'In the tunnel! There's a carrot growing!'

Her whole body sighed, and she lay back. Then she smiled and looked at me. 'Well. That *is* good news.'

I'm sure I sat there all day, watching that tiny speck of green to see what would happen next. Mam fetched a chair for me, and a blanket, even though it was warm in the tunnel. Within a week, there were rows of tiny plants pushing their way through the soil, and I guarded them as if . . .

Well. I was going to say, 'as if our lives depended on it,' which they did. I don't think I realized that at the time.

The plants insisted upon living, through the storms and high winds, through the days Mam and I were too ill to go out and tend them. I spoke to them, of course, because I like talking and because I felt like a father to them all in some small, silly way.

And here's something else that was silly. I felt guilty when it came to reap what I had sown. Pulling the potatoes and carrots from the soil, washing off the dirt in the stream, taking the big sharp knife to them. These plants had taken so long to grow, had lived when so many other things had died. I loved them, and I didn't want them to cease to be.

'I thought you'd be happy to be eating the things we grew!' Mam said as we stood in the polytunnel one day, the gardening fork already in the soil, ready to harvest the potatoes. 'You grew them yourself! You've done so well, Dyl.'

I swallowed and swallowed and swallowed, trying my best not to cry. I didn't want to admit it to Mam, didn't want to spill tears over something I knew was so stupid.

Mam sunk down to her haunches and touched my cheek. She smelled like the mint in the garden. 'It's probably hard. Eating them when you've worked so hard to keep them alive.'

I nodded, knowing that I'd cry if I tried to talk.

'Well. We've read the books haven't we, so we know to keep some for planting next year. We're going to collect the seeds from this year, and plant them next year. And the same the year after that, and the one after that. It's like . . . Like their children. We'll make sure that there are new ones every year.'

That made some sort of sense, but it still felt like betrayal. I knew that Mam had killed some animals for us to eat since The End—rabbits, a few squirrels—whatever got caught in the traps. But this was so much worse. I hadn't known the animals.

'I don't want them to die.'

Mam nodded. 'I know, sweetheart. But they're not like us, Dyl. They don't feel pain. They don't know what's happening around them. They're only plants.'

I'm still not sure that I agree with that.

The tears came when we ate those potatoes, after baking them above the fire for an hour. Inside the skin was a mix of chives, mint, and sage—herbs that I had grown—and salt, and a tiny amount of rabbit meat that was left over from last night's dinner. And I cried, a weird kind of crying, because the shape of my face didn't change and I wasn't breathing quickly or anything, but there were hot, fat tears running down my cheeks.

Mam reached out to hold my hand, but I shook my head. They were happy tears. I was seven and I had created food, and somewhere, in my little boy mind, I knew who I was, and who I was meant to be.

Rowenna

I think that I should write Dylan's story, because I don't see him often enough. That is, I see him all the time—we're never apart—but that is what makes a person invisible, seeing them every day. People fade in one another's company.

Dylan Llywelyn Williams, because I wanted to call him Llywelyn but I wasn't Welsh enough and I wasn't middle class enough. He was born in a white room in Ysbyty Gwynedd, the hospital in Bangor, on a Tuesday in January. Eight pounds and an ounce, though they'd stopped counting in pounds and ounces by then. Pitch-black hair, that shade of black when the sunshine falls on a blackbird. Shiny and smooth.

He was born scarred, the forceps leaving tidy curves on the side of his head. I was shocked by the brutality of the doctor's pulling, his effort and exertion feeling like something that didn't belong in a hospital. I had expected him to slip into the world, but the reality was complex, violent, and awful. I felt as if I had been gutted.

I was stunned by the gracelessness of birth, by the lack of peace. Giving birth was like being beaten up.

His father wasn't there. A friend of mine, Ella, was meant to come, but she wasn't answering her phone that night. So I was alone until Dylan arrived. I was alone from the start.

Being was very different before The End.

There had been a time, when he was a little baby, where he had been remarkable to me. His tiny fingers, the way he sometimes smiled in his sleep. The lovely weight and warmth of his body in my arms, and the brand-new buzz of the ego of parenthood. His smile when he focused his eyes on my face and smiled with recognition. His moaning cry when I'd put him down to make tea or go to the toilet. And when he was finally on his feet, his fat little arms around the legs of my jeans, anchoring me.

We used to pretend that there was martyrdom in having children, that we were putting ourselves to one side in order to serve our offspring. But people had children just to give their own lives purpose. To ensure that they had a good, worthy role in life. Before The End, having someone who was completely dependent on you was a good thing. It's an inhumane thing now.

Having children is the most selfish act possible.

We were always a team, Dylan and me. Us against the world, a two-man army with no arms except for an all-terrain buggy and Thomas the Tank Engine and tax credits. There was no one else left for me, not in the village, and I didn't want to leave my job and Gaynor for the bright lights of Bangor or Caernarfon.

Jesus. I was so lonely.

Friday nights, when the house was warm and cozy and Dylan was in bed, red-cheeked with exhaustion and smelling like soap and talc and milk. Sometimes, I'd have a glass of wine, but opening a bottle for one seemed wasteful and so it was usually just hot chocolate or a cup of tea. Rubbish on telly, or misleading posts of perfect lives on Facebook. A bit of tidying, a few messages to a few friends. And although I had it all—a warm house, a healthy son, a job I liked—the feeling was always there, that cruel, edgy feeling. I was waiting to be tired enough to go to bed. Giving my evening to a screen that couldn't see me. Spending my life watching other lives.

I was bored.

I can't tell you that my own children were different, without admitting that I was, or am, too. Shyness was in my very bones, a silent, still kind of girl, the sort of girl who is in your class throughout school but you never remember her once you leave. Of course, there are reasons for this, dark shapes in my murky early years, but I won't write about that. Not everything should be noted and remembered.

•

He was not like the other children. That was probably my fault. There was something anxious about the way he held himself, something shy about his movements. In a village and school and world that were desperate for attention, Dylan wanted nothing more than to be invisible.

He was someone else after The End.

Everyone is different, of course. But Dylan changed immediately, at the very beginning. After three days with no electricity, he stopped asking for screens. He started going out to the garden before I woke up in the mornings. After ten days, I stopped worrying that someone would come and steal him, and I allowed myself to believe that he would be okay on the lawn and under the hedges.

He was too young to help me with building the polytunnel—but he did help, and was helpful. And then with weeding, planting, and watering when we started growing food. Between games of racing Matchbox cars and making monsters out of plasticine, my son would collect firewood and scour the fields for mushrooms, and he transformed from an anxious little boy to a big boy who knew that he had a purpose, a job.

There is nowhere to hide in this new world. No

respectful distance between people, so no space for lies. I know exactly who Dylan is. He is strong but sweet, wise and tough. Sometimes, he is too silent, and he looks out across the mountains or out to Anglesey, and his mind is on things I don't know about. His mind is his only hiding place.

He's tall—taller than me—and the sun has browned his skin and has burned a red tinge into his dark hair. Big eyes, deepwater blue, and a square chin that says he will be handsome one day. Too thin, of course, but the tight muscles under his skin are enough to ensure that he doesn't look ill.

His front teeth are crooked, only very slightly, one overlapping the other ever so slightly, just like . . .

God help me.

That's the only thing he has inherited from his father, I think, the crooked front teeth, imperfect and lovely. When I allow myself to think about it, they remind me of long-ago smiles in the light of early morning, a mouth that was full of kind words and hopeful promises.

One day, one rare joyful day when he was just breaking into his adolescence, wiry black hairs starting to push through his chin like shoots, I watched Dylan, my almost-man, as we dug new trenches for the potatoes, his muscles too thick for a young man, his shoulders broadened with the labor of his work. And the sun was shining like a glinting blade on the sea behind him, and all the meek colors of nature seemed vivid because I was having a rare, happy, lovely day.

'You're so handsome!' I said, knowing that, in this world where appearance didn't matter, my son's beauty still made me proud.

Dylan straightened and turned to look at me and he grinned, a child's grin in a man's face. 'Hey, do I look like my dad?' he asked, a straight question, no edges.

And suddenly he wasn't so handsome anymore, and the colors not so bright around us, and the sea was just a cold, gray expanse of nothingness again. I didn't reply, but I let it drain the joy from everything. I turned back to my work.

I knew he wouldn't ask again, and he never has. His greatest fear is the withdrawal of my smile, and so my stony face has become my greatest weapon. He will never pluck up the courage to ask about his father again. He will never be brave enough to ask where Mona came from. He will not push me on anything, because he knows how cruel I can be.

I have an arsenal of coldness within me, ready for the questions I will never answer.

Dylan

Mona has a bit of a cough. That's how Mam says it—'a bit of a cough,' something and nothing. We're sure to catch it too, she says, because coughs spread like damp on walls. There's not much you can do about it.

But in the meantime, Mona won't settle. She's not sleeping, and she doesn't want to be put down at all. It's odd, because she doesn't seem to be happy with Mam or with me, but she doesn't want to be without us either.

Mam ties her to her stomach with the sling and carries on as if nothing is wrong.

When I was little, for a few years after The End, I would drink pink stuff out of a brown bottle when I was ill, and it tasted odd, sweet, like a thousand honeysuckles at once. But the pink stuff has long since run out, and we use the bottles for pickling, even though they're only tiny. They have white plastic tops that are perfect.

I'm worried about Mona, because her cheeks are so red and her eyes look all weird and lazy. But Mam says that Mona is strong, that it's only a cold. She says I'm a worrier, and she doesn't understand where I get it from, when we have nothing at all to worry about.

Last night, when we were sitting on the lean-to with a tarpaulin above us to keep us from getting soaked in the rain, I asked Mam, 'Why do people believe some books, but not others?'

'What?'

'Well, they believe in the Bible, but they don't believe Harry Potter.'

Mam's forehead creased. 'They're completely different. The Harry Potter books are novels.'

'Yeah, but the Bible has a story too. So why are we meant to believe in one but not the other? Because there are some very good lessons in Harry Potter. And *Cider with Rosie*. And *Lladd Duw*.' I knew she hadn't read *Lladd Duw*. It was a Welsh book, and I don't think she would have liked me reading it if she knew about the horrible things that happened in it. It was brilliant.

Mam raised one eyebrow.

'Seriously, Mam! I don't get it.'

'Neither do I, really. I don't know why, Dyl. Maybe you should treat every book equally and decide which ones you think are sacred.'

Our taste in books is very different. Mam reads quickly and reads the same ones over and over—The Brontës, Kate Atkinson, Bethan Gwanas, who writes about women like her but in the world that was before. I think Mam likes remembering that there were other women like her. She doesn't read that much Welsh, but more than she used to . . . Sometimes she mouths the words silently when she reads, and I always hope she'll read out loud so that I can hear what Welsh sounds like again, instead of just reading it in books. She loses herself in books, even though she's read the same ones tens of times before. I read slowly and read the same book straight after I've finished it, so that I can memorize it in my mind. Sometimes I read the same book eight times, straightaway. I know most of *Bury My Heart at Wounded Knee* by heart, and some parts of *Y Gemydd* by Caryl Lewis, and the opening pages to *The Kraken Wakes* by John Wyndham. I recite them to Mona whilst I'm working, and she listens, even though she doesn't always understand.

Even though Mam does sometimes talk about the world before The End, I think I learn more about it from books. She talks about how fast everything was, and how everyone had so much of everything, but the books say so much more. Mam says there's not so much killing as there was in Llwyd Owen's books, and no one is as sad as Morrissey's autobiography, but she doesn't know that it's those things that are interesting to me.

Were people like this with one another before The End came?

Like they are in the books—bickering and arguing over the smallest things, friends with some people but not with others? Some of the books are about mothers and children falling out, and living whole lives without seeing each other again—did that ever actually happen?

But the weirdest thing for me is something I can remember, I think, from the time before The End. They don't talk about it in the books, but it's there, unsaid, in everything. I asked Mam about it last night.

'People used to pass each other before The End, didn't they?'

'What do you mean?'

'Out on the street, or in a shop or wherever. People passed each other without saying anything. Without looking at each other.'

Mam shuffled a little closer to me. It was cold, but we were dry under the tarpaulin. 'Do you really not remember all that?'

A half-memory. But it feels so odd now that there's no one left, just Mam and Mona and me.

'Yes. Hundreds of people every day,' said Mam. 'In

the shop and in the garage and on the street. It meant nothing.'

'I don't know how the world could be like that.'

Mam pulled her hood down and looked at me. Her eyes were lost to the darkness, but I knew which expression she was wearing. 'What would you do, Dyl, if someone turned up here tomorrow?'

'It'd be brilliant!' I replied, as if I'd never dared imagine such a thing, that there were other people left except for Mam and Mona and me.

'And would you take them in? Give them a home and food?'

'Of course I would!'

'But what if there was—I don't know—four of them? And not enough food for you and me and Mona and four extra people? What would you do then?'

'I'd make it work. More planting. More polytunnels.'

Mam was silent for a long time. 'You've got a good heart, Dyl.'

'Maddau i ni ein difrwader,' I said, and Mam looked at me questioningly—the Welsh was too complicated for her to understand. I translated. 'It means, "Forgive us our apathy."' I thought about that imaginary family of four, wandering from place to place, looking for a home.

'You know your Bible,' said Mam, who doesn't.

'It's from a poem by Aled Lewis Evans. Mona likes it when I recite it to her. She likes the sound of it.'

'Of course she does,' Mam sighed. She's funny about the Bible, and anything that sounds like it.

The rain slowed and stopped. 'It's so perfect, this silence,' said Mam.

And we went back into the house and put the kettle on the fire to make a cup of nettle tea. Mam was reading a Welsh novel for older children which she had read dozens of times before. She sunk into one of the chairs with it. I went back to *Afal Drwg Adda*, the autobiography of a writer called Caradog Pritchard, because the man in it wrote about whizzing around on his bike, and I liked to imagine what that was like, to have so much to do and so many places to go. So many destinations.

'Do you want a blanket?' I asked, and Mam shook her head. She looked very happy.

Rowenna

Yesterday, Dylan asked me what Wylfa meant. I swallowed a few times, because I wanted to push that word right back down my throat, right back down deep into me. In the end, I said, 'Haven't you looked it up in your dictionary?'

He said that he had, and that there was nothing. And I asked if he'd looked in the Welsh one too, and he turned away and thumbed through the pages. Then he looked up, the confusion knotting his brow. 'Wylfa—beacon, or lookout point.'

I forced a smile. 'Pretty isn't it. The sound of the word.'

But it isn't pretty, not really, not to me.

Wylfa was the name of the nuclear power plant on the other side of Anglesey. I never heard an uglier, crueler word.

•

About six weeks had passed since the electricity had gone. Six weeks is a long time, long enough to get used to a new life. No one, no one at all, had turned town the little road that led to our house. There were only four people in our lives—Me, Dylan, and Mr and Mrs Thorpe.

There were signs that something awful was about to happen.

We were sitting on an old blanket on Mr and Mrs Thorpe's lawn. Well, Susan and I were sitting, and David was at the bottom of the garden with Dylan, by the pond. Dylan was kneeling in front of a dictionary, and they were trying to learn the proper Welsh words for the creatures they could see. *Madfall, malwod, morgrug.* I wondered why David Thorpe hadn't learned Welsh before—he seemed so keen to collect the words now.

Suddenly, they were everywhere. Slugs, on the lawn, on the path, on the blanket.

'Bloody hell!' David leapt onto his feet.

Everyone jumped up. We watched the hundreds of fat, wet slugs dotting the lawn between Dylan and me. He felt so far away.

'Mam . . .' Dylan said, sensing the grotesque wonder of this occasion.

'It's okay, Dyl,' I lied. 'They can't hurt us.' But I didn't know if that was true.

'But it's scorching hot!' David exclaimed. And about half a minute later, his wife replied, her voice as heavy as an ending.

'Exactly.'

I didn't understand straightaway. Slugs don't come out in good weather.

My mind didn't work like that back then. But I did get it, after a while, as I watched the slugs slowing and stopping and drying up, their ends curling, their skin turning to tongues of leather.

The slugs had chosen to die.

I looked up at Susan, and she looked at me. She was a pretty woman, in that quiet, still way aging middle-class Englishwomen can be. She wore a tiny cross on a thin silver chain around her neck; her hair a silky ball on the nape of her neck; narrow, long hands with small tidy nails. Her husband was kind and talkative, but this woman, Susan Elizabeth Thorpe, who was born in Thanet in 1943, a wife to David; a mother to Jonathan and Peter; a history teacher; secretary to the local branch of the Women's Institute—she was clever. She understood so much more than the others, in her own silent stillness. And when Susan looked at me that afternoon, a field of dried slugs marring the smooth perfection of their lawn, I knew.

'We'd better go home,' I said, scurrying across the

grass towards Dylan and trying to pretend that there weren't slugs bursting under my soles with every step. I grasped Dylan's sweating hand. 'See you later.'

I had only reached our garden gate when Dylan pulled on my hand and yelled, 'Mam!' And I heard it, quiet to start with, as quiet as a whispering voice in the night. Then louder, and louder, like a brewing argument, and the shadows, then, amassing on the horizon, a blackness coming from above Caernarfon.

Birds.

All sorts—seagulls and thrushes, magpies and pigeons and songbirds. A cloud of them flying south, their wings creating the sounds of panting breath, then the sound of chattering, then like an engine above us. Enough of them to block out the sun and make us cold. David and Susan stood on their lawn, hand in hand in old age, the flickering shadows thrown over them like an old film. I picked up my son, though he was too big and too old for that, and held him tightly. Dylan stared at the birds, watching the beautiful creatures leaving this place.

(Last year, whilst reading the Old Testament on some ugly, rainy day, Dylan looked up and asked, 'Is a dove a bird? Like, Noah's ark's dove?'

'Yes.'

An old shadow clouded his face and made him look

like a little boy. 'I remember those birds leaving, all that time ago.')

The cloud of birds passed and disappeared over the hills to the south. There was a second of eerie silence, and then it happened.

A roar. A vibration. The world's most powerful thunder. Something angry possessing the world, something screaming, something dying. I think it lasted for about a minute, but it could have been for longer, or shorter. It faded slowly, quietened gradually. And although the sound had come from everywhere, had filled the air and the earth and our bones, we all knew from which direction it had come—we all stared in the same direction.

Anglesey.

The cloud, then, rising far away, like sudden weather closing in. Susan shouted at me across the garden. 'Get in the house! Now!' As I ran towards home, Dylan restless in my arms as I held him too tightly, I heard David asking his wife, 'What? What is it?'

And Susan, her voice light as a breeze, tight as a fist. 'Wylfa.'

Dylan

I haven't written about Pwyll for a while.

This is what happened.

The hare started to trust me, but that happened slowly, slowly. I started trusting him too. A part of me was still afraid of him, and that weird dead face that always stared at me from the back of its head. But I've read enough to know that people aren't the same on the inside as they are on the outside.

(In *Folk Tales of Wales,* volume 2, by Endaf Hughes, there's the story of Melangell, the saint that saved a hare from a hunter. The story goes that Melangell herself turned into a hare, her soul stuck inside a darting, gray creature. It's not impossible that she is this one, with the second ugly face.) I decided not to see the things that were wrong with him.

I would sit in the shed, as still as I could, with a piece of carrot or a cabbage leaf in my hand. Pwyll didn't come anywhere near me the first time, but the second time, he creeped out of his hiding place behind the paint tins and crouched there, looking at me. And then, slowly, he inched towards me, before springing forward and taking the food from my hand.

Mam wouldn't have understood, especially as food was scarce, with nothing left over to feed a pet.

I can remember touching Pwyll for the first time.

He was smooth and soft, and even though he was still scared of me, he knew I wouldn't hurt him. I didn't touch his second face, because that would feel a bit like touching a scar. In a few weeks, Pwyll was leaping onto my lap to be fed, and then he'd settle to sleep on my lap, enjoying the rhythm of my strokes on his back.

It's lovely to have something small and soft to love.

There are always things to do. Trees to cut down or soil to weed, something to fix or tidy up. But I took an hour of every day to spend time with Pwyll. Sometimes, if he lay a certain way across my chest, I could feel the purr of his heartbeat, fragile under his ribs.

One cold October morning, I took Mona to see him. She was wearing her blue coat and her fleece hat, and her hair was curling in little ringlets above her collar.

She stared at Pwyll, and then grasped my leg nervously. She saw a monster, not a little animal, and the shed felt too small for the three of us.

'It's okay, look,' I told her, kneeling by her side. 'He's Pwyll, and he's sweet. Look!'

I fetched a slice of carrot from my pocket. Pwyll padded forward and took it from my hand and started to eat it. A peal of laughter escaped from her mouth. 'Carrot!'

'Yeah, he likes carrots! And he likes being stroked, look.' I smoothed my hand down his back, and Mona sunk to her haunches, and extended her hand to stroke Pwyll's long ears.

'There you are,' she said, mimicking Mam's soft bedtime voice. 'There you are.'

We went to see Pwyll every day after that, unbeknownst to Mam. Mona wasn't old enough to keep a secret, but she wasn't old enough to tell that much, either—she didn't have the words. Our visits to Mr Thorpe's shed were ours alone. I'd started to use the garden of Sunningdale for planting (rhubarb, beets, turnips, chives), and so Mam never suspected anything.

Mona fell for the weird creature. She never tired of playing with him, feeding and petting, speaking her half-language with him (*Eat it ALL; Good Pwyll; Sit down, cariad, sit down),* occasionally laughing at him. Once or twice, she'd fallen asleep on the hard wooden floor of the shed, Pwyll curled into her like a doll.

Then, one day, I was taking some of the chives to

put them in the kitchen, Mona beside me with strict instructions to stay nearby and play with her ragdoll. I heard a scream from beside the shed, and there was Mona, her ragdoll face down in the dirt, the shed door ajar, and Pwyll having fled for freedom as soon as he was given the chance, without giving a second thought to the people who had thought themselves his owners.

'Pwyll!' yelled Mona, with streaming eyes and nose, her voice scratchy and broken. 'Come home!'

That is the story of Pwyll. Mona still asks about him sometimes, and I tell her all about his life after he left us, a life with fairy friends and a new family consisting of stoats and merpeople who lived in Llyn Cwm Dulyn. Llyn Cwm Dulyn is the big dark lake in the valley, and if you look closely the water is clear but from far away it looks murky. It's pretty but the mountains around it always make it feel like you might drown. Mona listens to my stories wide-eyed, her thumb in her mouth. She believes it all, and sometimes I am thankful that she accidentally released Pwyll. A life within four walls isn't enough for a wild animal, even if it is half monster.

Rowenna

You can't contain air. You can't stop it from seeping.

I shut all the windows, of course, and drew the curtains. I lay in bed, Dylan by my side, the duvet over our heads and the smell of sleep almost smothering us.

I thought we were going to die in that bed, Dylan and me. The cloud would come and kill us both, just by breathing into us.

I held my son tightly, and felt our bodies exchanging heat. His hair smelled like moss, and I could smell last night's bonfire on myself. Earth and fire. And as this was to be the end, I started to sing. The only hymn I knew, in my mother tongue, the words flickering like a faulty memory over my tongue. "Calon Lân," the song about a clean heart, the song of rugby crowds and funerals and joyous choir practices in the vestry on a summer evening.

I don't know why I chose that hymn. I knew plenty of prettier-sounding pop songs, but that was the sound that escaped from my mouth when I thought we were dying.

Dylan was stiff for a while, fear making his muscles tight. But after a while, a merciful exhaustion overcame him, and he relaxed. He extended a small hand and rested it on my cheek, and said with a small voice that was as gentle as his clean heart,

'Mam.'

We both fell asleep. There are worse ways to end.

When I awoke, most of the cloud was gone, and the smell of plastic filled the house, like the times when I'd left a Tesco bag on the hob by mistake, or when Dylan left his Action Man on top of the fireplace. He was still asleep, so I got up carefully and peeped through the windows. The day was drawing to its close, and wisps of the cloud were on the hills, just like the mists that sometimes draw in from the sea.

There was a soft knock on the front door. I padded downstairs quickly, not wanting to wake Dylan.

Mr and Mrs Thorpe stood on the doorstep, their coats on even though it was still warm. Susan was wearing makeup—I'd never seen her like that before, rose-lipped and misty eyeshadow on her lids.

'We're off,' said David, and I swallowed, feeling the weight of the words I had been expecting for a while. A few weeks earlier, these people had been nothing but chirpy voices on the other side of the garden walls, tight smiles as I passed in the car. But after The End, they were my only friends. The only people I could talk to and feel like something of normality was left.

'To find your sons?' I asked, trying to keep the emotion out of my voice. 'I'm sure you'll be back when . . .'

The rest of the sentence hung mutely between us.

'Not to look for the boys,' said Susan, something tight in her voice and eyes, something forever locked away. She was trying to make this look easy. 'We won't see you again, Rowenna, but we've left the key under the mat. Take anything you need. Move in, if you want to.'

She looked beyond me as she spoke, failing to catch my eye.

'Where are you going?' I asked.

David smiled sadly. 'We're heading towards Wylfa.'

I looked from one to the other wildly. 'Wylfa! But it's . . . You'll be killed!'

And Susan raised her eyes to mine finally, and said, 'Yes.'

I can't remember the rest of the conversation, only that an awful normality overcame us all. No, I wasn't to wake Dylan to say goodbye to them, but Mr Thorpe wanted him to have all his tools from the shed. No, I needn't go outside to wave goodbye to the car. The engine was already running, and no one wanted to make a fuss. Neither of them hugged me, and they didn't lean over to kiss me. I didn't offer a hand to shake, and I didn't beg them to stay.

'Goodbye, Rowenna,' said Susan with a smile, and turned towards the car. This quiet, graceful woman had worn her church clothes for her final journey.

'Rowenna,' said David. 'When we've gone, I want you to go into my shed. On the top shelf on the right, there's a long black case containing a shotgun. There are three big boxes of cartridges by its side. Take them and keep them under your bed.'

'What! I don't want a gun in my house!'

'Do this for me. This one thing. Just in case you ever need it. Please, Rowenna. I'm going to die this afternoon, and knowing you have this protection would put my mind at ease when I go.'

I nodded silently, and David Thorpe awarded me with a big, wide smile, a smile that reached his eyes. 'You have the heart of a warrior, Rowenna.'

'But I don't want to fight,' I replied. 'I want to live.'

Before they slipped into the car, Susan turned to me and waved. 'Diolch,' she said, the word of thanks a whole language on her tongue. And then, they had gone, leaving an empty world behind them.

Rowenna

Yesterday, I had to go to the garden of Sunningdale to fetch a turnip. Dylan has been planting there and the soil is good. I'd caught a rat in the trap in the back field, and it would make a good stew with some turnip and rosemary.

It was a beautiful day, cold and frozen but crisp and clear, my breath making clouds around my face, proof that I was alive. Dylan and Mona were in the bottom field planting trees. Dylan says that it's important that we plant trees, because we'll need them for firewood in fifteen or twenty years' time. Twenty years! How can a boy so young think so far ahead?

I'd just walked through the gate into Sunningdale's garden when I saw it. A shiver ran through my body as I saw the thing that wasn't even trying to hide, not trying to run away.

It was a hare, I think, or two hares, because it had a second ugly, flat face on the back of its head, empty-eyed with a cruel little mouth. It was foul, an abomination.

It was obviously not right in the head either, or it would have scampered away as wild animals are supposed to do.

I only had the gardening fork with me, but it was enough, and it was easy. The monster didn't move away as I moved closer to him, and the metal spokes of the fork sliced through his flesh with barely any effort from me. The creature twitched a few times and stilled.

Though we usually threw our rubbish into the heap at the end of the garden, I buried the hare in the garden of Sunningdale, then covered the earth with dead leaves to hide the grave. It was only a small thing, but I did not—and do not—want the children to see terrible creatures. I can't protect them from the big things, but some small things can be kept from them.

There are hideous beasts around since the cloud passed over us.

I can't remember when the sickness started, only that Dylan and I became horribly ill, bedbound. I was absolutely certain that we were going to die.

I'm not sure what that explosion was. Maybe an accident in Wylfa Power Station, but maybe not. Perhaps it was a bomb in Bangor, or on the bridges to Anglesey. I know nothing about the effects of radiation, so I can't imagine how much of that poison seeped into our bodies, nor how much of it is still there.

I was wise. Made strong, perhaps, by David's faith in me, I decided to behave like a woman with the heart of a warrior. When the sickness first started to churn in my stomach, I strode back and forth between the house and the stream in the back field, filling bottles, saucepans, pots, and placing them around my bedroom. If we were going to be sick, I'd have to make sure that we didn't dehydrate.

After a few days, my bedroom started to smell like death.

Dylan and I, naked and sweating between violent bursts of sickness. Pain, everywhere—in our muscles, in the marrow of our bones—and then, nothing, no feeling at all, both us of hovering on the marches of life. It was a half-existence, with only flashes of reality disturbing my sleep.

A blade of light cutting in between the curtains.

Wet bedsheets, and not knowing whether it was sweat or piss or vomit. And Dylan, his body still and pale, pale blue. He was dead, and all I could do was clutch at his naked body, and yell and cry and sleep and hope that I, too, would die.

When I awoke, Dylan was warm again, and breathing. For the first time in days—weeks, maybe—my son and I looked at one another.

'I had a dream that you were dead,' I said. 'It was terrible.'

'Water,' said Dylan weakly, and I reached for one of the bottles I had dotted around the room. In the depths of our awful sickness, I had forced water into our mouths.

'It was a terrible, terrible nightmare,' I said, believing wholeheartedly that it was not a nightmare, but that my little boy had been reincarnated in his mother's filthy, stinking bedroom, his clean heart having cleansed all the poison from his blood.

It wasn't over, of course. It took months for us to be able to hold our food down properly. And the mouth ulcers! Filling our mouths, huge open sores that tasted like rotting meat and were sometimes bad enough to make our teeth loosen and fall out.

I don't know how long had passed since the cloud passed over us, but one morning, in the big bed, Dylan sat up and started making dog shapes with his fingers in shadows on the wall. I decided then and there that we would survive.

In my shaky, weakened, skinny state, I opened all the windows and doors. I pulled the sheets off the bed and decided that once I was strong enough to drag the mattress downstairs, I would take it out of the front door and burn it. I opened a tin of red kidney beans, and

Dylan and I sat on the doorstep, sharing them, one plain bean at a time.

'Do you think that the birds will come back?' Dylan asked.

'Course they will,' I replied firmly. 'Everything will come back in the end.' And I remembered what Mr Thorpe had said about the gun, and thought I'd have to go and fetch it soon.

Dylan

Mona has been coughing for a while, so I offered to stay here with her whilst Mam goes to Llyn Cwm Dulyn for a wash. I think it's too cold for washing, but Mam said that she could smell herself.

I've made a fire, and Mona has fallen asleep in the armchair, so I'm going to take the time to write about the conservatory. It still makes me smile, years and years later.

It was before Mona was born, and Mam decided, one day and out of nowhere, that we were now allowed to go to the empty houses in Nebo and take whatever we wanted.

I didn't know that I wanted anything. By then, we had two polytunnels, and were growing enough to feed ourselves. The traps were catching us plenty of meat. And Mam had been so sure that stealing was a terrible thing and yet, there we were, breaking into people's houses and taking what we wanted. No one was around.

It was as if everyone had gone on holiday and had forgotten to come home.

I got new clothes that fitted me perfectly, a bike, a new mattress for my bed, a few books. Gloves, a scarf, socks. Wellies. But I had bigger plans.

I was looking at the conservatories on the houses. They were plastic, ugly white plastic with huge windows. I didn't like their look at all, like big ugly blemishes on the friendly faces of old houses—but I wanted one. I wanted one more than anything.

And so I got one.

I wasn't sure that it was going to work, and I felt a bit guilty for stealing a whole room for someone's house, although that someone was long gone. It took months for Mam and me to do it.

Firstly, we had to choose the right one. There were six conservatories in Nebo, and four of those had brick walls at the base, so they were no good to us because it's hard to move a brick wall. There was one with wood and windows, and one with PVC. Mam said it would be easier to take the wooden one, because there were screws to unscrew and we knew were we were with stuff like that. And it was a better fit for the space we had beside the lean-to.

Fair play to Mam. I was only little then, so she had to help with everything, especially the carrying from the village, and the building after we got home. We didn't know about roofing and slates at the time, so we made a roof out of tarpaulin, which wasn't as good as it could have been. I put a proper slate roof on it once I learned how to, a few years later.

It wasn't perfect for a long time, that conservatory, especially the way it fitted onto the house. It leaked for the first year or so. But it's perfect now, after years of trying and correcting and improving.

Of course, we don't use it as a place to sit and relax. That wasn't the point. It's full of plants that need to be kept warm, like tomatoes and zucchinis and peppers. In the winter, we keep a small fire going there, in an old coal bucket we stole from one of the houses in Nebo. We keep it by the door so it doesn't get too smoky, but it's still good. The conservatory is never cold.

That's the thing I'm most proud of. Mam knew how much I wanted a conservatory, so she made sure we got one. And she let me do most of the work, even the dangerous things. She knew I needed to learn that I could do things on my own.

The conservatory was just the first step. I went to get the second one, the plastic one, a year or so later, and building it was easier than I thought. I was more confident this time. It was a perfect place to keep the seeds and grow the tiny seedlings in spring. Mona has made a tiny den under one of the benches, with a big blanket made out of rabbit fur. She strokes it as if it's alive.

After I built the second conservatory, we needed a cool, dark place to store the potatoes and onions and carrots and turnips and apples that would keep us going throughout winter. So I built a big store in the back garden, half of it underground, with a big wooden roof. There are shelves—some built by me, some stolen from Nebo. I haven't put anything on the walls, because the exposed soil is good for keeping everything cool.

After the food store, I built a dry stone shed to store the firewood. There's enough in there to keep us going for years.

And then, after the wood store, I decided to build an outhouse, because we were used to doing our business in holes in the field, but Mam was expecting Mona by then, and she was big and deserved to be able to sit down properly within four walls when she needed to go. We dig a very deep hole and place the chair over it (an old chair from one of the posh houses in Nebo, with pictures carved into the back, and a place name and a date too. I cut a hole into the seat.) The outhouse is made out of wood, and can be moved, along with the chair, to another spot when the hole in the ground gets full.

After the outhouse, I decided to try and build my own polytunnel. It was difficult, because the first two came from kits that Mam bought before The End. But I had some clear tarpaulin, and wood to make a frame. I thought it would be simple in comparison to all the other things I've built, but it was by far the most difficult—large and awkward, determined to succumb to the wind. I almost gave up and blamed the poor quality of the tarpaulin. But I didn't, and by the end of the following year, Mam and I didn't have to worry about food anymore. We didn't run out of a single thing.

Sometimes—often, actually—I stand at the bottom of the garden and look at all these things I have made, the buildings and the plants and the food—and I feel like a man, not a boy. And I don't want to change a single thing, I don't want this to end. I fit here, now.

Rowenna

Does it sound awful? The End? Losing it all, society collapsing, everything I knew in pieces?

I was never so satisfied.

It felt like falling, to begin with—a lack of help and care and support, plus insecurity about the most basic things, health, food, home.

There is no energy left to worry about anything else, and the exhaustion of the physical work we have to do to stay alive means we sleep at night, instead of staying awake, worrying about things we can't change. Things are so simple now, and so easy to love.

The morning mist like old ghosts at the bottom of the garden.

The peal of Dylan's laughter as he reads something funny in one of his books.

The flowers that are yet to come, and my faith in them even when the weather is at its cruelest.

I think about how things were before The End, and

it doesn't feel like me, in those memories. That girl, silent and afraid of the world.

I used to go for walks with Dyl when he was little, my iPhone snug in my pocket, creating perfect images to share online without actually having to share anything of myself. And Dylan, since infancy, bewitched by screens. The real world disappointed him, lacking the beginning, middle, and end of an episode of *Fireman Sam* or *Thomas the Tank Engine*. We lived without silence. The sound of the telly or radio was a constant companion, but there was a terrible, noisy silence about the way we used to live.

Once you stop listening, you begin to hear.

The chaos of rain patterns on the window. The wind singing like a siren or whispering like a lover. Waking in the morning and knowing, without looking, that it had been snowing—you learn to hear its thickness on the ground outside.

And you see the beauty too—things are so much prettier than they were. And yet, they're not. Everything is the same, but we can see it all now.

People like us don't usually live in houses like this.

Women like me lived in squat, gray, ugly mid-terrace two-bedroomed houses with damp walls and noisy neighbors. Or, as I did before I had Dylan, in one of the council flats above the playing fields, with brown stains on the ceiling and the thick smell of piss in the lift. I hated that flat. Downstairs lived a middle-aged couple who fought and fucked loudly, and the window of my living room looked out towards Talysarn and the slate quarry. I was utterly alone. It was magnificent, that view, like an ever-changing canvas of blue and white and purple on my wall, but I couldn't see beauty.

If I'd have been living there when The End came, there instead of here . . .

A bloke came into the Silver Scissors one afternoon and greeted Gaynor as though she was his mother. I never saw anyone treating Gaynor like that, not before or after that, and there was something about the way they both shut their eyes tightly as they held each other that made me like that man.

He was the only son of Nancy Parry, one of Gaynor's longest-standing customers, and he was here to cancel her appointment as she'd gone to a nursing home in Felinheli. He sat by Gaynor as she combed her customer's hair, and his soft voice somehow managed to fill the shop and still sound gentle.

'We don't want to sell the house, really, but I don't like the thought of it being empty either. And I don't really want to rent it out, what with all the bother of insurance and tax and all that.'

He was very tall, this man, too tall to fold neatly into a chair. I think he was around fifty years old, but his smile was boyish, and his slightly stooped walk made it look as though he was trying to hide himself.

'Can't you rent cash-in-hand to someone you know, and not bother with all those rules?' asked Gaynor, and I happened to look up at that second, and caught her eye in the mirror.

Gaynor saved me in so many ways.

'Um,' I started, and the man turned to me and smiled, a dazzling smile that showed his front teeth, slightly crooked like old gravestones.

It was a small house, but it was in the middle of nowhere and it had a garden, and although I was lonely sometimes, it was a peaceful sort of loneliness. The rent was the same as what I paid for the flat, because the electrics were old and dangerous, and the windows were rotting and draughty, and the kitchen had been there since the sixties. It was close to the huge TV mast in Nebo that could be seen for miles and miles around, Anglesey and Caernarfon and Llŷn. At night, a string of red lights lit up the ugly metal pole like shining poppies. I could see home from far away whenever I drove back at night, and sometimes I wondered whether the man was watching from Anglesey, looking at the string of pretty red lights that pointed towards heaven.

He came every month to collect the rent, his car full of child car seats and teddy bears and empty pop bottles. I never asked about his people, and he didn't ask about me.

I really did think that I loved him.

In the beginning, he was drunk with the idea of me, the quiet, young woman who lived like a ghost in his mother's house. *I'm going to leave her. I'm gonna move in here with you, Row.* He'd leave the house and I would be able to smell his aftershave and his smokes and his sweat long after he left.

He watched the swell of my belly, sat in my bed talking about names, and sometimes, not often but sometimes, half-promises would be sighed from his crooked teeth. *It's you I want to be with* or *I'd give the world to be able to . . .*

By the time Dylan was born, I'd lost faith in him. I couldn't hate him, because hate is a strong emotion, and I didn't have any strong emotions left for him. I pitied him and his gray life, his lack of courage, and all the dull days he lived.

He never came in anymore when he collected the rent.

The last time I saw him, about a fortnight before The End, he said, 'I just didn't want to hurt anyone.'

But he knew that Dylan was watching cartoons in the house, and he didn't ask to come in to see him.

I'm almost sure that he's dead now.

His name was Sam.

Rowenna

'Mona won't remember life before The End,' said Dylan as he watched his little sister sleeping, curled up like a cat on the sofa. 'Because she wasn't here. Her life is completely different, because she wasn't here in the olden days.'

I was surprised to hear Dylan say that, because I thought that he knew that Mona was dying.

She was only two, my little girl, two and a bit. She was born in the eye of one of the worst storms of the season, a storm that ripped trees up from the roots and shattered one of the windows of Mr Thorpe's shed, the glass ground fine as sugar. Dylan said that Shakespeare had written about the way the earth shook like a coward when Owain Glyndwr, the Welsh hero, was born—maybe the baby would be a hero too. I remember thinking how odd it was that my son was quoting Shakespeare as I was in labor with his sister.

Her arrival was so different to his. The flow of clear liquid from my body seeped into the soil as Dylan and I made sure that the polytunnels were secure before the storm that could be seen amassing above the Irish Sea. I stood still, the trickling down my legs warm to the touch.

'The baby's coming,' I said calmly, and Dylan looked at me and nodded. By the time I finished, I was having pains every so often, but Dylan went to look at the traps and to fetch water from the stream.

I sat on the sofa with my favorite book, a Welsh novel that I'd read a hundred times, and scribbled the translation of the words I didn't understand in the margins. It was called *Creigiau Milgwyn*, and it was an old-time love story that always made me feel warm and safe. I read through the pains.

By Chapter 5, I was light-headed with pain.

'Go and get the tarpaulin from the lean-to, and put it on the floor,' I told Dylan when he came in from outside. I didn't want to ruin the towels with my blood.

And that's where we were, my son and I, waiting for the storm and for the baby. He didn't hold my hand, but he did make me smile.

'It's better than it was in the hospital, isn't it? You were on drugs and off your head when you were giving birth to me. At least you'll remember this time! What shall we call the baby?'

'In the olden days, they used to name the weather,' I said between contractions.

'What? With people names?'

'Yeah . . . Like Hurricane Katrina, and Storm Iris.'

'Imagine giving bad weather such pretty names! Can we call him Daniel if he's a boy?'

'Like the one in the lion's den in the Bible?'

'Like Daniel Owen.' Daniel Owen was a Welsh novelist, long, long dead. Dylan had a tower of his novels on the floor by his bedside.

I was never so glad of the fact that I'd raided that library.

It was easy, in the end, that birth—my body knew what to do, when to push, when to pause. The little girl slipped from my body into her brother's hands and opened her black eyes and took her first breath. Dylan kissed the baby's head, and then he had the stain of my blood like lipstick on his mouth.

'Mona!' I said, the storm still trying to break into the house. Because Mona was the old name for Môn, Anglesey, the isle we could see from the lean-to. 'Let me feed her.' I felt her weight in my arms, and love, like a new electricity, shot through my bones, my engorged breasts, through the pain between my legs. God almighty, that miracle of Mother Nature, always ready to love without restrictions, without complexity.

It would have been odd, before The End, for a young son to help his mother at the birth of her child.

For him to be so enchanted by the miracle of breastfeeding. And for him to then reach for the blackened frying pan in order to cook the placenta.

'Don't use it all,' I warned as he sliced the flat pad of meat with the sharp knife. 'I'll make a soup with half of it tomorrow, there's plenty of carrots and onions to go with it, and you can fetch some nettles.'

And we sat, this brand new trinity, Dylan and I eating the afterbirth as if it was steak and my daughter sleeping in my arms, her mouth still puckered at my breast.

'Dylan Llywelyn and Mona . . . what?' I asked when we had finished eating.

'Mona Rowenna,' Dyan replied firmly.

'No, no. Greta. Mona Greta.'

And that is who she is.

Dylan

Mona is still ill, and she doesn't want to be put down at all anymore. She won't sit on the sofa, playing with her dolls, and she wouldn't collect stones and flowers in the garden as Mam and I work. She wants to be in our arms all the time.

Mam sits up with her at night, so I take her for most of the day, and carry her in the sling as I walk or tend the plants. I tie the sling so that she sits high on my back, and she can rest her head on my shoulder if she wants to sleep. Sometimes, the coughing takes hold of her, her little body shaking with the force of them. And then she becomes quiet, and is exhausted by them.

Today, I returned to Nebo, my sister on my back. To a house on the outskirts of the village, a house I had been in several times before, but I go back there time and again because of the wall of photographs they have. I don't know why I like them so much, or why I take some of them home to hide in the pages of books.

The house is large, one of the biggest in the village,

and it looks quite new, as if it was built just a few years before The End. It's tidier than most of the houses, and lighter.

I let myself in through the back door, and took off my shoes. I don't usually take my shoes off in people's houses.

'House,' said Mona softly from my back.

'Yeah. Big posh house,' I agreed, and walked through the house, enjoying the softness of the carpet beneath my feet. I knew where everything was—a big double bedroom in the front of the house, and three smaller bedrooms at the back of the house, one belonging to a teenage girl. I walked into her room—Kate, it said on a small wooden sign on the door—and sat on her bed.

I like going to Kate's room. She has an entire wall of people in frames—of Kate herself, Kate and her parents, Kate and her friends. She is a tall, slim young woman, with long, straight-combed hair, pink lips, and brown eyes. She smiles in every photo, a wide smile, a lovely smile that makes her eyes wrinkle at the corners.

In the corner of her room, she has a wardrobe, crammed too full of jeans and dresses and fluffy jumpers. Her school uniform hangs from the back of her bedroom door. She has a long bookshelf, but they're not very good books. At one end is a collection of lovely little perfume bottles.

Her phone and laptop chargers are still plugged into the wall.

Her schoolbooks are on her desk—Kate Francis, 10B, written in fat little letters on the covers.

Kate Francis is so, so pretty.

I don't know what it is, that feeling I get as I stand in front of the photographs on the wall, staring at the life of Kate Francis. Her clothes and books and friends, every one of them frozen forever on this bedroom wall. They're probably all dead now, of course, and anyway, they'd be about twenty-five by now if they'd have lived, adults like Mam. But they're young forever in this room, still and smiling in this perfect house.

What would it be like to be one of the boys in the photos?

Laughing with a group of friends, knowing people who weren't related to you. Choosing to be friends, and sometimes choosing not to be. Get a girlfriend, maybe. Someone whose eyes wrinkled at the sides when she smiled, like Kate Francis.

Mam doesn't know that I come here on my own.

I say I'm looking for nettles or blackberries or dandelions for us to eat, but on the way, I come here. I like the way the silence feels thicker, and the carpets are bouncy, and that it feels like I might hear a car pull up outside any moment, the family spilling out of it after just popping out shopping. Here, I am closer to the time before. I could almost spin around in Kate's bedroom to see that she's caught me there, horrified and fascinated at the things I do in her room when no one is looking.

I don't know if my body is doing what it is supposed to do, and there is no one I can ask about it—certainly not Mam, in case her face becomes hard and flat, like a slate. I have read in books about the throbbing of my body, so I think that bit is normal, but I'm not so sure about the way my mind has a kind of buzz inside it when I think about Kate's skin, and the way that sometimes I can't sleep because all the guts and muscle and bones inside me feel like they need another person. The books don't talk about that. Maybe it's a sickness.

'Tired,' said Mona, and rested her head on my shoulder, I could hear her breath scratching in her lungs.

I walked down to the kitchen, and opened the cupboards, although I'd pilfered what I could from them before. There was nothing there for us—plates, saucepans, too-old tins of meat and fish. Mam and I had taken from everything else.

But there was one thing we missed, because this morning, I opened the bottom drawer in the kitchen, where there was a tidy pile of folded-up tea towels. Underneath those, there was a long rectangular package, with the word MARZIPAN written on it in bold letters in gold.

'Are you awake?' I asked, and Mona raised her head. I opened the packet, and smelled the contents. It was like sugar, and something else, something warm. Something in me remembered that smell.

I tore off a corner of the marzipan and gave it to Mona.

'Don't want it,' she said.

'But it's special. It's new.'

She took the small yellow ball from my fingers. I took a bite from the rectangle of marzipan in my hand.

It was wonderful—too sweet, but full of taste. And I suddenly remembered where I'd smelled it before—in the Silver Scissors, where Gaynor used shampoo that smelled exactly like marzipan on the hair of all those old women.

Gaynor! I hadn't thought of her for years.

'More,' said Mona, and I smiled. She had been off her food for days.

'What do you say?'

'More, please.'

And Mona and I ate half of that packet of marzipan on the way home, and felt guilty when we only had half of that scented, sugary treat to give to Mam.

Rowenna

In the old days, living was so easy.

So easy that we used to play a game with death. Who could play chicken with our lives and get away with it? Who could smoke the most, drink the most, eat the most before getting ill and dying? And even if we did get sick, it rarely mattered—a constant flow of medicine and answers and healing was available at the village surgery.

Over the years, Dylan and I have needed a doctor, even the hospital sometimes, a team of white-coated specialists to smile at us and treat us. Like the time Dylan got so ill that he was shitting blood and seeing things that weren't there. Or the time that I slipped from the roof when I was trying to fix a leak and broke my ankle. I still walk with a limp. Mona's birth, and the fever she caught when she was six months old.

We've learnt, Dylan and me, to use moss to absorb blood when a cut is large and exposed. We know that steam is the best thing for a cold or cough. We've learned that stinging ourselves with nettles heals a surprisingly long list of ailments and illnesses.

But Mona will not heal now. I can see it, and I think that Dylan sees it too. Something in the way she holds herself, the loose movement of an old person in her toddler body. There is a slowness to the blinking of her shining, tired eyes. She still drinks my milk, but she has no appetite, and she's too thin.

It's been there since her birth, that threat of her death—I can see it in the slowness of her movements, something odd in the shape of her head, the thickness of her tongue as she speaks her few words. I don't know if Dylan has noticed, but it is there. She is not normal. There's something there, some weakness.

Her cough is like an engine at night, like something that can't be coming from her little body.

I spend the nights with her on the sofa, holding her up because she can't sleep when she's flat on her back. Sometimes, the heat of her is sticky on my skin, and sometimes she feels as cold as slate. Last night, I opened my shirt and undressed her, and wrapped us both in the blanket, skin to skin, her small hands on the nape of my neck, her fists loose.

And because I have nothing but words for her, in all my inadequate strength and weakness, I started speaking to her in the very blackest moments of the night.

'There you are, Mona, cariad bach.' She moved her hand a bit, tightened and loosened her fist, and then touched the bones of my shoulder with the pads of her fingers. 'You'll be better when the good weather comes. Of course you will. And the flowers will come back, the llygad y dydd and the pabis Cymreig and the dant y llew.' The Welsh names bloomed on my tongue.

'Mam,' said Mona in a gentle voice that hadn't said enough words.

Dylan

On the last day, I put her in the sling, but in the way that I used to, so that she was tightly bound to my chest, not my back. She had hardly slept, and so I lifted her from Mam's arms in the morning.

'Go to bed,' I said to Mam.

'I shouldn't.'

'Yeah, you should. You have to.'

Mona looked at me as I changed her clothes, stared at my face in a way she'd never done before. Not examining, but letting her eyes rest on my face. I put her coat on, and placed her in the sling, and then I wore the big coat and closed the zip over both of us. She could still see, but she was safe and warm.

I took her to our old places.

Round the garden, and to the back field, the polytunnels, the conservatories. *This is where the potato flowers come up, isn't it, Mona? And this is where we grow the turnips. And that's where you fell and cut your knee...*

To the garden of Sunningdale, where she liked

rubbing her hands in the herbs and then sniffing them deeply. I lifted a sprig of rosemary to her nose, and my sister took a small breath, searching for the trace of her summers in that smell.

Over the fields to Nebo, where we'd found a buggy for her, and blankets and tiny clothes. The kitchen where we'd eaten that marzipan a few weeks ago.

And then, Llyn Cwm Dulyn, the huge black lake, still and cold. It wasn't the right weather for paddling, but I put my arms around her and sung into her hair, and thought about the night that she was born. Her little mouth on Mam's breast, and all that she brought with her when she slipped into the world. Hope. Newness. And that something, that huge, wonderous nameless thing that made Mona unique.

She looked up for a moment, and turned her eyes to the lake, then the mountains, and then over to Caernarfon and Anglesey and the endless sea. Then she rested her head on my chest again, and fell asleep.

I'll never forget that noise that Mam made. Howled, wolflike, as if she was a creature that knew no words. Out in the garden, the day drew to a close, and Mona was dead.

•

Mona Greta was buried today, under the apple tree on the lawn, wrapped warmly in her pajamas and her favorite blanket. Having to cover my sister in soil was the worst thing in the world, and Mam was half yelling, half crying as she kneeled down in the grass. I was trying not to look at her, because something inside me felt as if it was churning with hot, thick blood. But I did look at her, and her face was wet and red and ugly, and a horrible guttural sigh came straight from my lungs.

As I shoveled soil into the grave, each load of earth feeling heavier than the last, I saw an arrow in the sky shooting over our house. I hadn't seen a single bird since they all escaped in one black cloud all those years ago, and here they were, silent, graceful, returned. Today is the day my sister was buried, and today is the day the birds came home.

'Canada geese,' I said quietly, watching them disappearing towards Caernarfon.

Tonight, Mam and I sat on the lean-to in our coats, even though it was cloudy and starless. Mam was very, very still, and quiet, her face as cold and closed as slate.

'I'm going to make a gravestone with her name on

it,' I said, feeling like I was speaking to no one. 'And I'm going to carve in it, *You know the way to the place where I am going.*'

Mam's eyes flashed, and there was something dangerous in them, something new.

'The Bible?'

'The Book of John. Mona liked the Bible.'

Mam sighed deeply. She looked into my eyes, and spat out her words as if they were poison in her mouth. 'And where the hell is your God now?' She climbed down from the lean-to and disappeared into the house.

For a second, and for the first time in my life, I hated her. Her voice and face and scent, the fact that she was there every bloody time I turned round, her secrets and history. Her lack of mercy as she ridiculed my faith. It only lasted for a moment, that feeling, but I've never hated anyone before. It's almost as strong as love, but nowhere near as strong as faith.

I let myself think all the things I usually kept locked up in my head. *What are your secrets? Who is Mona's father? Who was my father? Who is your father? Why did you bring me into this world when things were always teetering at the edge of The End?*

I hated her.

Soon, I could hear her sobbing in her bedroom.

I thought about Pwyll, that ugly freak of a hare, and

the way Mona used to fall asleep with him curled in her lap. Mam didn't even know of Pwyll's existence. Now that Mona was gone, no one knew but me.

Everyone has their secrets.

Rowenna

I have to write down who her father was, and I'm not sure why. Maybe because that will make her more real, this little girl whose existence was never registered, the girl who never went to a park or a school. My daughter, whose face was never captured on an iPhone camera. Mona Greta, my little baby girl.

It was a rainy day in February, and some snow was clinging to the sheltered corners of the fields. Around two years had gone by since The End, and almost that long since Dylan and I had seen another human being. Mr and Mrs Thorpe felt like a long-ago dream. Everything before that—work and school and Gaynor—felt like they belonged to someone else's life.

As usual, Dylan began his day by filling the bath with water from the stream. He had started planning a system which used an old pipe to pump water into the house, but he hadn't done it yet. He'd carry bucketfuls of water into the house every morning. He was not an eight-year-old child in his mind. He was a worker.

That morning, I decided to walk the mile or so down to the main road with Mr Thorpe's tools in my backpack. Dylan and I were building a huge dark box to grow mushrooms, and we needed a large, flat lid. I thought that one of the road signs would be perfect—one of those that showed the drivers that there was six miles to Caernarfon, or twelve miles to Bangor. If they were too big, a speed limit sign would do, or a P for parking.

No traffic had been on this road for years. Everyone else in the world was dead. So I stepped out onto the A487 that, years ago, had been a constant hum of cars and lorries. By now, moss and grass and weeds had grown over the tar.

I had started to pull down the sign which read

Nebo 1
Cesarea 1/2

from its pole. I sweated as I hit the metal with a heavy mallet, and I swore loudly, but I was enjoying it too, because I knew that I'd succeed.

And from the corner of my eye, I saw the slightest movement.

A man was cycling towards me down the A487. I swore, of course, and raised the mallet above my head, ready to strike. The man leaped off his bike when he saw me, and we both stood still, staring at one another.

If I'd had the gun, he wouldn't have lived to utter a single word.

He looked like Jesus Christ.

Long, tangled hair, a beard hiding half of his face. His body too thin, his jeans too short, and a dirty white T-shirt. Huge brown eyes, calf eyes, childlike eyes.

'Go away!' I snarled, almost scaring myself by the roughness of my voice. I sounded like an animal.

Jesus Christ raised his hands, showed his palms, as if I was pointing a gun at me.

'You're here!' he said in a voice that hadn't spoken in a long time. 'You're here!'

'Where did you come from?' I asked, the mallet still above my head.

'I thought I was the only one left!' he said. 'I live by Porthmadog. In the middle of nowhere. I don't know whose house it is, but they've gone.' He looked up at the mallet in my hands, and he said, 'Please. I'm not going to hurt you. I'm just so happy to see another person.'

After a few seconds, I lowered the mallet. Jesus Christ smiled.

'Are there people in Porthmadog?' I asked, and the man shook his head. 'I think there's a man somewhere around Penrhyn, I think, because I've seen smoke. But Porthmadog itself is dead.' He shook his head, as though the fact was still a shock to him. 'How about you?'

'Up there.' I nodded towards home.

'The girl under the mast,' he smiled, as though he didn't know that the pretty lights on Nebo mast had stopped working years ago.

'I haven't seen anyone in years. Although, I do have a boy. I'm not on my own.'

The man grinned. He was handsome, I think, although such an idea felt redundant after The End. 'A boy! How old?'

He was called Gwion. We sat in the middle of the A487 for a while, facing one another over the faded white line, a soft drizzle slowly soaking us. He didn't know any more than I did about what had happened, or what was happening, or what would happen next. He only knew that gangs of people had been fighting at the very beginning of this, battling over food and fuel and medicine. By now, they had either killed each other or moved away to somewhere else. Perhaps, Gwion said, life was normal in Cardiff or London. The fact that society had fallen here didn't mean it had everywhere. All the people had gone somewhere—they couldn't all have died.

'Do you really believe that?' I asked.

Gwion shrugged. 'I don't know. I can't decide what to believe, nor what to hope for. Does humanity just start again now? Or are we waiting to be saved?'

I had longed for these kinds of conversations, without even knowing it. Of course, Dylan was good company, and could speak to me as an adult now, almost. But he barely remembered life before The End. None of it was real to him.

I stood up after a while. 'I'd better get on with this.' Gwion nodded, and without discussing it, came over to the road sign with me in order to help. Before long, the sign was down, and was ready to be dragged home as a lid for the mushroom box.

Gwion reached into his backpack. I took a step back, my instincts telling me to be careful.

Gwion stared at me, and was still for a while before he said, 'I'm not going to hurt you. You shouldn't lose faith in people like that.'

And he reached into his bag and pulled out a bar of dark chocolate.

'A month past its sell-by date, I think—I'm not exactly sure what date it its.' He handed it to me. 'For your boy.'

I didn't know what to tell him. 'I haven't got anything to give you.'

'I don't want anything. I find nice things sometimes.

It makes me happy to think that a little boy will be getting a bar of chocolate.'

Gwion was a thief, going from empty house to empty house looking for food and clothes and plants for the garden of his stolen house. He'd been into hundreds of homes, he said, but I was the first person that he saw.

'Well, alive, anyway,' he added then as I slipped the chocolate back into the back pocket of my jeans. 'I think the cloud killed most of them.'

I hadn't thought about the cloud for a while, though I'd always known that Dylan and I would not have survived if it wasn't for the water I'd forced down our throats when we were ill. I wouldn't have had the energy to reach the stream when I was at my weakest. We would have died of dehydration.

'Thanks for . . .' Gwion started, and took a few seconds to think about what he wanted to thank me for. 'I thought everyone was gone. I didn't think I'd ever hear another person's voice.'

And even though I was hardened and cold and suspicious, I couldn't help but smile at Gwion. Jesus Christ on the A487.

He must have worked out which house was ours, because of the polytunnels and the new plants and, of course, he would have noticed the smoke curling in ribbons from the chimney when it was cold. Every couple of months, I'd find a gift on the doorstep—a box of sugar lumps, or a pot of Asda Italian Mixed Herbs, or, on one fine and wonderful day, a bar of old-fashioned soap, the orange type that smells like the past.

One night, almost a year after we met on the A487, I was drawing the curtains before going to bed when I saw him there, standing behind the garden wall, his bag on his back. I immediately flew into a panic—what if Dylan woke up and saw him? Dylan knew nothing about Gwion! And yet, I couldn't deny the wave of joy that I felt when I saw him there. The kind of joy that had been missing since The End, the jolting kind, a lovely surprise.

'You can't come in,' were my first words to him. 'I don't want Dylan to see you.' He was wearing a shirt this time, a blue shirt with small, pearlescent buttons. It was starting to get dark, and the end of the day complemented him perfectly. He looked lovely.

'You're still here! Brilliant!' said Gwion with a wide smile. 'You're surviving! It's amazing, Greta!'

I don't know why I lied to him about my name when we first met. Maybe everything felt too personal in this new world, and my name felt like the only thing that belonged exclusively to me. Dylan called me Mam. No one said Rowenna anymore.

He'd come to me every three months or so,

bringing a gift each time, and sometimes with a nugget of information too. He'd seen a dead whale on the beach in Morfa Bychan, and a family of deer in the midst of the weeds in the car park by Tesco in Porthmadog. And then one day, 'I've checked the houses in Nebo for you. There's no one in them. Just don't go into the bedrooms whose doors are shut because, you know. The cloud.'

'Why are you telling me that?'

'Look. I know you don't like the thought of stealing, but I'm sure these people would want you to have their stuff.'

The moral argument was already formed on my tongue, but I knew he was telling the truth. The village of Nebo was only half a mile away, and I knew that there would be clean blankets for me and Dylan, saucepans and dishes, perfect slates to fix our roof with. I'd been sleeping without a mattress for almost three years, and the thought of the luxury of being clean and dry was almost too much to bear.

'Thanks,' I replied, knowing that this was the next huge small change in our lives—breaking and entering, theft, surviving on the crumbs of other people's lives. No, not surviving—we were already surviving. But I wanted more. Just a bit more.

'Are there books?' I asked.

'God yes! Loads of them. They deserve to be read, Greta. They deserve to be appreciated.'

And that is what we did.

•

I won't write about the rest. About his hand reaching out to hold mine in the twilight of my garden on one cooling night, or about how it felt to sweat with a man that smelled like the earth. I won't describe the heat of his smile in the polytunnel as the snow fell outside like the ashes of a faraway fire, his soft thumb on my cheek. I won't talk about succumbing, finally, to the temptation of the key that was kept under the mat outside Sunningdale and letting ourselves into Mr and Mrs Thorpe's house, lying in their bed that was damp and dusty and felt as soft as a cloud in heaven. And I won't mention—or allow myself to remember—the small tattoo on his foot, lit by the soft glow of the moon through the window and a flickering candle on the bedside table, the letter M printed simply on his pale skin. I didn't ask about it, but I pulled my thumb over the letter, and Gwion stirred in his sleep, and opened his eyes and blinked, his blue eyes made black by the night. I stroked the M on his foot, my touch asking the question I wasn't brave enough to voice. He was silent, then he swallowed a few times, before saying in a tight whisper, *I was a dad, before all this. I can't.* And he couldn't. There was nothing more he could bring himself to say about that.

But it's important that I do write about Gwion, because it would be so easy to misunderstand our relationship. A woman exchanging her body for bars of soap and bars of chocolate. A business transaction in a world that is brimming with want. But that is not the kind of relationship that created Mona. No man was ever as happy to see me as Gwion was, and I never felt such an honest, primal, true attraction. I think that love is better suited to this world than the one before The End came.

I don't know what happened to him. Perhaps he'd been spying on the house, and had seen my belly, a big firm ball under my T-shirt, as I'd been pinning the clothes on the line or chopping firewood. Maybe he was dead, murdered, or struck down by illness. Perhaps he just got fed up with waiting for an invitation into the house and having to see me in the polytunnel or in Mr and Mrs Thorpe's ghost house.

And maybe he wasn't really called Gwion, and maybe he hadn't been a carpenter before The End, and maybe he didn't live in a little stolen home by Porthmadog. Maybe he had tens of women like me that he visited, women that were always half waiting to see the shape of his body at the end of their gardens at the end of the day. But I choose to keep the faith. If Gwion could be here, I choose to believe that he would. And that he would have known his daughter and he would have loved her. And the things we believe in, the things we have faith in—we have all made the choice to believe.

Rowenna

Once I decided that it was okay for us to steal from the houses in Nebo, everything was easier and more difficult.

'What made you change your mind?' asked Dylan as we walked across the fields that very first time. It was almost winter, and Dylan was about nine—after Gwion started to visit me, but long before I became pregnant.

'I think it's time.'

'But why? Why is it time?'

I stopped dead, unreasonably frustrated with my son, and painfully aware of why that was. I was keeping the existence of Gwion from him, and in some weird, messed-up way, I felt that I was being unfaithful.

I stared at my son, who was thinner and more muscly than a nine-year-old child was meant to be. Dylan smiled at me, his father's crooked teeth in his mouth plucking a note of an old memory within me.

'Dyl. What do you want, more than anything in the world?'

His smile faded as he seriously considered this question. 'Anything?'

'Anything at all.'

Dylan thought. I remembered his last Christmas before The End, the terrible mountain of plastic and electronics which was somehow meant to prove my love for him.

'A conservatory,' he replied firmly. 'One that stays really hot, and stuck on to the house, with a little fire in it.'

I couldn't help but smile at him, even though he was utterly serious. His hands were rough and hardened, but his touch was gentle—the hands of an instinctual gardener. 'What do you need to do that? Because we're doing it, Dyl. Look for the things you need in Nebo, in the houses and gardens. And we'll take them home, and you can do as you like with them.'

His eyes widened. 'Really?'

'Really. But you have to promise me something. Don't go into any house before I've had a chance to see it, okay?'

'Okay.'

He was too young to see a dead body.

There's something about other people's houses.

The first and most obvious thing is the smell. Years

had gone by since anyone had lived in these houses, but their ghosts remained in the subtle scents—washing powder or cigarettes or polish. Everyone had left as if they'd just gone to work—a dirty mug in the sink, bills on the doormat, bold red lipstick on the shelf in the bathroom. It took months for us to explore the houses of Nebo, dragging our spoils home in brown or green wheelie bins, and then keeping those too because they were good for catching rainwater. We got:

- a double mattress for my bed, and a single one for Dylan;
- tens, if not hundreds, of tins of food, most of them edible;
- sweaters, coats, socks, shoes;
- needles and thread;
- books.

I saw dead bodies for the first time. Five or six of them—maybe more—I wasn't counting. Old people and young people and middle-aged people.

The first ones are the ones my mind keeps returning to.

•

It was a council house, a mid-terrace. There was a blue BMX in the front garden, as if its owner had thrown it aside when he heard his mother's voice calling him in for tea.

They were in the big double bed in the front bedroom, bones in pajamas by the time I found them—a Man U T-shirt in the arms of a lavender-colored bathrobe. Their hair was perfect, the mother a bleached blonde (had I been the one to dye her hair?) and the son was dark.

I paused as I walked in. Dylan was in the garden, examining the BMX, the possibility of having his own bike slowly enchanting him. I could hear him on the street, playing with the bike chain and trying the brakes.

I stared at the dead bodies of mother and son and listened to Dylan outside and remembered our sickness after the cloud came.

This woman in the lavender bathrobe—she could have been my friend. The boy—maybe he was like Dylan, and they could have played football and shared ownership of the BMX. He could have been his friend.

I stepped into the room, and somehow, I suddenly remembered Psalm 21, and was surprised that I could recall every word. I recited every single word and didn't believe any of them. You don't have to believe in order to recite the psalms. There's comfort in the rhythm of them, especially in Welsh. I sometimes read them at the end of the day when my mind is too exhausted to catch the thread of a novel.

I looked in her wardrobe, and saw the little details of who she was, dust like a lace shroud over everything. Pink lipstick. A bottle of perfume called NRG; a hair-brush with a few golden threads between its bristles. Spare change. A card with a picture of a sunflower on the front, with untidy words scrawled inside. *Hope it all went well. I'll come and see you and Nathan soon, after things have settled down. Lots of love, M xxxxx.* It was a thoughtless message, scribbled quickly to catch the post, perhaps, but it meant something to the blond-haired woman who had rotted in her bed. She had brought it up to her bedroom, her most private and personal space, instead of leaving it on the windowsill or on the fridge.

I wondered where M xxxxx was now.

I opened the pink lipstick, and smeared it over my thin, cracked lips. Had she been pretty, the blond woman? What did her voice sound like? Did she read to the little boy in the T-shirt before he went to sleep at night? Did she smile at him when he came out of the school gates?

There was a pile of clothes on a chair in the corner of the room, waiting to be ironed.

As I stole a saucepan and old clothes and salt from the house, I promised myself that I would return to this house, would dig a hole in the back garden, and give this two-person family a proper burial. But in the end, I didn't have the heart to do it. They looked happy in bed together, silence like an extra blanket around then.

Dylan

It's a long slab of slate, a foot across and three feet high, and it was once a part of a fence separating one person's field from another's. These slabs are placed close together, like huge blackened teeth jutting from the earth and tied together with wire to stop the sheep getting through. We call them crawia. Someone put them there. Someone made the effort to heave hundreds and hundreds of slate slabs from the quarry and half buried them in the earth, used them to split up the mountains into parcels of land.

I stole the crawia and left a gap in the fence, before heaving it home on a wheelbarrow and placing it flat on Mona's grave. It would have been easier to carve out the letters in the shed, where it was dry and silent, but I preferred to carve right there, with Mona fast asleep underneath me in the earth.

It is nine days since we buried her, and things have changed. Mam and me don't talk properly, not like we used to. She doesn't come and sit with me on the lean-to at night, and she doesn't read either. She does a few necessary things—gardening and fixing and cooking—and then goes to bed without saying goodnight. And I tend the fire and read the essays of T. H. Parry-Williams, an old writer who lived on the other side of the mountain. Sometimes I sit on my own in one of the polytunnels or on the lean-to. I think about Mona, and sometimes I smile and sometimes I cry until I feel sick. I'm not sure why, but sometimes I think about Pwyll too, and I cry about him. But I always cry silently, in case Mam hears me.

I am longing for something, but I'm not sure what for.

I've been using a hammer and chisel to write out the letters on the gravestone and taking my time so that it's done properly. Her name in large letters—MONA and then GRETA underneath it. And then, I had to think of something new to put on, because after what Mam said about God, it didn't feel right to put a quotation from the Bible on there. I want to remember Mona, not the argument.

I sat on the doorstep, thinking of what to put. There were thousands of books in the house, and I knew half of them off by heart, but nothing sounded perfect.

A few geese flew overhead. I haven't seen crows or gulls or songbirds yet, but they must be coming.

And as I thought about how far they fly, about all the places they belong to, I thought about how Mona belonged here, only here. This place was her life, and she will always be here, in a way, as long as Mam and I remember her with her feet in the stream and collecting blackberries from the hedges. That's how people live forever, I think, in the little memories in familiar places.

I went back to the stone and started carving.

Mae darnau ohonof ar wasgar hyd y fro.
T. H. Parry-Williams

I didn't know if Mam would be annoyed with me for putting Welsh words on the stone. She didn't ever speak Welsh to us, even when Mona and I played with both languages. But I thought she'd be okay with it, because it was her mother tongue, and I thought it suited Mona.

Pieces of me are scattered over the land.

It doesn't look like crawia now. It looks like a grave.

Rowenna

I haven't written anything for a long time. I can't write down all the reasons why. It feels like an unseen fog has surrounded me and Dylan since Mona left, and *The Blue Book of Nebo* doesn't hold the answers to all the unanswered things that hang between us.

It is months—I don't know how many—since we buried my little girl, and months since Dylan reached for this book and wrote anything down. He's a man now, and there's an uneasiness between us since my grief made me cruel. I know why he doesn't write anymore. He doesn't want this period of time to be noted, remembered.

I think about him leaving me.

That may be what's next. Dyl moving on from here, casually announcing that he's going to Nebo or to the back field to weed the potatoes, and never coming back. Maybe that's what's on his mind when I catch him gazing out towards Anglesey, or when he sits out on the lean-to in the rain. And yet I know, deep down, that he is too kind to leave me. I'm his responsibility. He is disgustingly, horribly bound to me. He does more than me to make sure we survive.

It happened again tonight, as it does some nights. I was drifting off to sleep then I heard her, her high, thin voice yelling, 'Mam!' A short, happy, joyful sound, and although I knew that I was dreaming, I sat up and looked around for her. I am always looking for her. I'll never be cured of this kind of madness.

I got up and walked over to Dylan's room. The door was ajar, and he was sleeping with his back to me, the blankets pulled tightly around him.

'I'm sorry,' I said quietly, and Dyl sat up straightaway.

'You okay?'

'Yes. I want to say that I'm sorry for everything. I love you very much.'

Silence stretched like time. There was so much more to say, but I hoped there'd be no need.

'Sometimes I think that I can hear her. In the middle of the night. Then I wake up and . . .'

Dylan nodded.

'And I don't like it when I wake up and I remember.'

'No. But we're okay, Mam.'

And then we both slept, and in the morning, things were very slightly better.

Rowenna

It only happened this morning. I'm still shaking. I've been like this all day. I'm doing my best to explain to Dylan, but the words all stick together like boiling sugar and I know I sound as if I'm losing it. *Itmeansthat . . . Iwasn'texpecting . . .*

He was chopping up firewood after spending yesterday dragging down the tree trunks down from the village using old chains. I was in the polytunnel separating and repotting the seedlings, watering them, and placing the pots in a row on the shelf. I was humming an old Welsh folk song to the rhythm of the chopping from outside. I don't know many Welsh songs, but that one was on an old Dafydd Iwan CD that Gaynor used to put on sometimes. Sometimes, Dylan and I would sing it like an anthem. I couldn't remember the real Welsh anthem, and anyway, the words were something about the land of my fathers, the land of poets and singers and brave warriors, and so it never made sense to us. It didn't sound like home.

The rhythm of the axe gave way to stillness. I waited for a moment, thinking that Dylan was fetching more wood to chop up, or taking a gulp of water.

And then I heard the yelling, and my son's footsteps thundering towards the tunnel. Panic tightened my throat. *The axe, the axe, he's been hurt.* But there was no blood on him when he came in, his eyes wide. He looked like a boy again.

'What?'

'Listen!'

And I listened, and heard nothing for a while, but after a while the sound started to creep in, rasping, a low moan.

'What is it?' Dylan asked, frightened. 'It sounds like the sky's being torn apart!'

I rushed past my son and stared up into the sky. It was far away, but it was loud because we were so used to silence.

'What? What is it?' asked Dylan again as he saw the black, waspish shape tearing its way over to Caernarfon through the empty blue sky.

'It's a helicopter,' I replied, and we stared at one another.

•

I am afraid.

Of the old world, the gray days of technicolor screens. People passing one another without saying hello. Ordinary lives. Helicopters.

Dylan

Mam has started to come to me in the evenings, when I'm sitting on the lean-to. We don't talk about the fact that we've been so quiet for such a long time, or that we're barely writing in *The Blue Book of Nebo* anymore. We can't find the right words.

We haven't talked about that night she said she could hear Mona calling out for her. I've read about the same thing happening to T. H. Parry-Williams. He wrote long ago about voices in the night, voices that weren't there but could still be heard, and I'm glad, I'm so glad, that this happened before The End, too. It's not just us. I haven't told Mam about what T. H. Parry-Williams wrote. She's had enough of Bibles and old books.

'I'd love a smoke now,' Mam said as we sat on the lean-to. Steam was coming from her mouth as if she really had a cigarette.

'I'd love some marzipan,' I said, remembering that day in Nebo with Mona, the taste of sugar and almonds in our mouths. And then, long ago, The Silver Scissors, and Gaynor, and marzipan-scented shampoo by the sink.

'I'd love to be able to pop down to Penygroes for a kebab,' said Mam. 'With garlic sauce. And loads of raw onions.'

'Would you really?'

'No,' she replied honestly.

The days before The End were threatening us both.

The helicopter, rasping its way through the sky in a huge ugly sheen of metal, its audacious racket shattering the noise of nothing. Then, nothing for days, and the endless circle of questions between me and Mam started to calm.

But what does it mean?

It means that there are people out there, and they're trying.

Trying to do what? Trying to get things back to the way they were?

I don't know, do I, Dyl. I don't know.

And then yesterday, the new sound, that was far, far worse than one helicopter. A screaming, like lots of babies crying together, like the wind wailing through a storm.

We were weeding the back field.

'Oh no,' said Mam, turning her eyes to the big road that's covered in moss and grass.

'What is it? Something in pain?'

'They're police cars.'

And they passed, far away, as if their presence made some sort of sense in this world.

'Shit,' said Mam, her slate-hard face pale and lined.

'What?'

'It's coming back, isn't it? The world as it was. It's coming back.'

I didn't want to ask, *Is that a bad thing?* because it was obvious that it was. But I hadn't expected her to react in this way. She looked lost, her life a spinning compass, out of control. And Mam is not that kind of woman. She is hard and strong and in control of everything.

'I can feel it coming back, like a cloud,' she said, and she hurried away in the direction of Llyn Cwm Dulyn.

Rowenna

The best things are . . .

Green shoots forcing their way through the warm earth.

Sunsets over Anglesey, blushing the sky like a shy lover.

Dylan singing when he thinks I'm not listening.

Seeing someone on an old bicycle on the A487 when I thought everyone had gone.

A full moon.

Mona's ragdoll on the shelf, and the lovely, painful memory of her little hand grasping it tightly.

A mute television thrown over the garden wall with the rest of the rubbish.

Soup, when Dyl and I have grown every one of its ingredients.

The absence of people, bustle. All the absences.

Life.

Dylan

'Do you think we'll be saved?' asked Mam tonight as we were sitting on the lean-to. She's been very quiet since we heard the police cars.

'We don't need saving, for God's sake,' I replied without pausing for thought. Mam reached out and held my hand.

'I'm bloody proud of you, Dyl.'

I smiled in the darkness. Her words made it feel as if there was another End in sight.

We were silent for a while, and then she said, 'I wasn't really me before, you know.'

'What do you mean?'

'Before The End. I was scared of everything. I always thought I was bound to mess everything up. But we've done okay, haven't we? You and me. And I had Mona, and I do my best.'

'Yeah,' I agreed. 'This is who you really are, Mam. You do your best, and we're okay. You're strong. Like a warrior.'

•

We sat in silence. I don't know what Mam was thinking about, but I was remembering all the brilliant things, like the polytunnels, and the first plants, and Pwyll, and Mona splashing in Llyn Cwm Dulyn, and all the stories in all the books. And our book, *The Blue Book of Nebo*, living amongst them on the shelf.

And Anglesey lit up.

A wave of light, like close-up stars, lighting one after the other, orange and white. Houses and street-lights blinking and waking up, as if they'd fallen asleep ten years ago. Civility and civilization returning boldly after a long long time away.

The lights of Anglesey grinned at us like a fiend.

'Are you okay?' I asked, and Mam squeezed my hand, her wet eyes sparkling in the new lights.

Acknowledgments

To my family, especially my loving and kind sons, Efan and Ger, whose patience I shall be forever grateful for.

To everyone at Y Lolfa, the Welsh Books Council, the Wales Literature Exchange, and the Eisteddfod Genedlaethol. Diolch.

To all at Deep Vellum, especially Jill Meyers, who edited this novel with sensitivity and thoughtfulness.

To my agent, Christopher Combemale at Sterling Lord, for all his hard work.

And to my parents, am yr holl gariad.

About the Author

MANON STEFFAN ROS is a Welsh novelist, playwright, and screenwriter, and she is half of the Welsh folk duo Blodau Gwylltion. She has written more than forty books in her native Welsh language. Her novel *Llyfr Glas Nebo* (which translates to *The Blue Book of Nebo*) won the Welsh Book of the Year in 2019, as well as the People's Choice Award and the prose medal at the 2018 National Eisteddfod. Her novels for children and young adults have won the Tir Na N'Og prize five times, and her novels *Llyfr Glas Nebo* and *Blasu*, as well as her play *Two Faces/Dau Wyneb* are on the Welsh curriculum for teaching in schools. Originally from Rhiwlas, a village in the mountains of north Wales, she now lives in Tywyn, a town by the ocean, with her two sons. Manon loves Liverpool Football Club, hiking, and cake.

PARTNERS

FIRST EDITION MEMBERSHIP
Anonymous (9)
Donna Wilhelm

TRANSLATOR'S CIRCLE
Ben & Sharon Fountain
Meriwether Evans

PRINTER'S PRESS MEMBERSHIP
Allred Capital Management
Robert Appel
Charles Dee Mitchell
Cullen Schaar
David Tomlinson & Kathryn Berry
Jeff Leuschel
Judy Pollock
Loretta Siciliano
Lori Feathers
Mary Ann Thompson-Frenk & Joshua Frenk
Matthew Rittmayer
Nick Storch
Pixel and Texel
Social Venture Partners Dallas
Stephen Bullock

AUTHOR'S LEAGUE
Christie Tull
Farley Houston
Jacob Seifring
Lissa Dunlay
Stephen Bullock
Steven Kornajcik
Thomas DiPiero

PUBLISHER'S LEAGUE
Adam Rekerdres
Christie Tull
Justin Childress
Kay Cattarulla
KMGMT
Olga Kislova

EDITOR'S LEAGUE
Amrit Dhir
Brandon Kennedy
Dallas Sonnier
Garth Hallberg
Greg McConeghy
Linda Nell Evans
Mary Moore Grimaldi
Mike Kaminsky
Patricia Storace
Ryan Todd
Steven Harding
Suejean Kim
Symphonic Source
Wendy Belcher

READER'S LEAGUE
Caitlin Baker
Caroline Casey
Carolyn Mulligan
Chilton Thomson
Cody Cosmic & Jeremy Hays
Jeff Waxman
Joseph Milazzo
Kayla Finstein
Kelly Britson
Kelly & Corby Baxter
Marian Schwartz & Reid Minot
Marlo D. Cruz Pagan
Maryam Baig
Peggy Carr
Susan Ernst

ADDITIONAL DONORS
Alan Shockley
Amanda & Bjorn Beer
Andrew Yorke
Anonymous (10)
Anthony Messenger
Ashley Milne Shadoin
Bob & Katherine Penn
Brandon Childress
Charley Mitcherson
Charley Rejsek
Cheryl Thompson
Chloe Pak
Cone Johnson
CS Maynard
Daniel J. Hale
Daniela Hurezanu
Dori Boone-Costantino
Ed Nawotka
Elizabeth Gillette
Erin Kubatzky
Ester & Matt Harrison
Grace Kenney
Hillary Richards
JJ Italiano
Jeremy Hughes
John Darnielle
Julie Janicke Muhsmann
Kelly Falconer
Laura Thomson
Lea Courington
Leigh Ann Pike
Lowell Frye
Maaza Mengiste

pixel texel

ADDITIONAL DONORS, CONT'D

Mark Haber
Mary Cline
Maynard Thomson
Michael Reklis
Mike Soto
Mokhtar Ramadan
Nikki & Dennis Gibson
Patrick Kukucka
Patrick Kutcher
Rev. Elizabeth & Neil Moseley
Richard Meyer
Scott & Katy Nimmons
Sherry Perry
Sydneyann Binion
Stephen Harding
Stephen Williamson
Susan Carp
Susan Ernst
Theater Jones
Tim Perttula
Tony Thomson

SUBSCRIBERS

Ned Russin
Michael Binkley
Michael Schneiderman
Aviya Kushner
Kenneth McClain
Eugenie Cha
Lance Salins
Stephen Fuller
Joseph Rebella
Brian Matthew Kim
Andreea Pritcher
Anthony Brown
Michael Lighty
Kasia Bartoszynska
Erin Kubatzky
Shelby Vincent
Margaret Terwey
Ben Fountain
Caroline West
Ryan Todd
Gina Rios
Caitlin Jans
Ian Robinson
Elena Rush
Courtney Sheedy
Matthew Eatough
Elif Ağanoğlu

AVAILABLE NOW FROM DEEP VELLUM

MICHÈLE AUDIN · *One Hundred Twenty-One Days*
translated by Christiana Hills · FRANCE

BAE SUAH · *Recitation*
translated by Deborah Smith · SOUTH KOREA

MARIO BELLATIN · *Mrs. Murakami's Garden*
translated by Heather Cleary · MEXICO

EDUARDO BERTI · *The Imagined Land*
translated by Charlotte Coombe · ARGENTINA

CARMEN BOULLOSA · *Texas: The Great Theft* · *Before* · *Heavens on Earth*
translated by Samantha Schnee · Peter Bush · Shelby Vincent · MEXICO

MAGDA CARNECI · *FEM*
translated by Sean Cotter · ROMANIA

LEILA S. CHUDORI · *Home*
translated by John H. McGlynn · INDONESIA

SARAH CLEAVE, ed. · *Banthology: Stories from Banned Nations* ·
IRAN, IRAQ, LIBYA, SOMALIA, SUDAN, SYRIA & YEMEN

ANANDA DEVI · *Eve Out of Her Ruins*
translated by Jeffrey Zuckerman · MAURITIUS

PETER DIMOCK · *Daybook from Sheep Meadow* · USA

ROSS FARRAR · *Ross Sings Cheree & the Animated Dark: Poems* · USA

ALISA GANIEVA · *Bride and Groom* · *The Mountain and the Wall*
translated by Carol Apollonio · RUSSIA

ANNE GARRÉTA · *Sphinx* · *Not One Day*
translated by Emma Ramadan · FRANCE

JÓN GNARR · *The Indian* · *The Pirate* · *The Outlaw*
translated by Lytton Smith · ICELAND

GOETHE · *The Golden Goblet: Selected Poems* · *Faust, Part One*
translated by Zsuzsanna Ozsváth and Frederick Turner · GERMANY

NOEMI JAFFE · *What are the Blind Men Dreaming?*
translated by Julia Sanches & Ellen Elias-Bursac · BRAZIL

CLAUDIA SALAZAR JIMÉNEZ · *Blood of the Dawn*
translated by Elizabeth Bryer · PERU

JUNG YOUNG MOON · *Seven Samurai Swept Away in a River* · *Vaseline Buddha*
translated by Yewon Jung · SOUTH KOREA

KIM YIDEUM · *Blood Sisters*
translated by Ji yoon Lee · SOUTH KOREA

JOSEFINE KLOUGART · *Of Darkness*
translated by Martin Aitken · DENMARK

YANICK LAHENS · *Moonbath*
translated by Emily Gogolak · HAITI

FOUAD LAROUI · *The Curious Case of Dassoukine's Trousers*
translated by Emma Ramadan · MOROCCO

MARIA GABRIELA LLANSOL · *The Geography of Rebels Trilogy: The Book of Communities; The Remaining Life; In the House of July & August*
translated by Audrey Young · PORTUGAL

PABLO MARTÍN SÁNCHEZ · *The Anarchist Who Shared My Name*
translated by Jeff Diteman · SPAIN

DOROTA MASŁOWSKA · *Honey, I Killed the Cats*
translated by Benjamin Paloff · POLAND

BRICE MATTHIEUSSENT· *Revenge of the Translator*
translated by Emma Ramadan · FRANCE

LINA MERUANE · *Seeing Red*
translated by Megan McDowell · CHILE

VALÉRIE MRÉJEN · *Black Forest*
translated by Katie Shireen Assef · FRANCE

FISTON MWANZA MUJILA · *Tram 83*
translated by Roland Glasser · DEMOCRATIC REPUBLIC OF CONGO

GORAN PETROVIĆ · *At the Lucky Hand, aka The Sixty-Nine Drawers*
translated by Peter Agnone · SERBIA

ILJA LEONARD PFEIJFFER · *La Superba*
translated by Michele Hutchison · NETHERLANDS

RICARDO PIGLIA · *Target in the Night*
translated by Sergio Waisman · ARGENTINA

SERGIO PITOL · *The Art of Flight* · *The Journey* · *The Magician of Vienna* · *Mephisto's Waltz: Selected Short Stories*
translated by George Henson · MEXICO

EDUARDO RABASA · *A Zero-Sum Game*
translated by Christina MacSweeney · MEXICO

ZAHIA RAHMANI · *"Muslim": A Novel*
translated by Matthew Reeck · FRANCE/ALGERIA

JUAN RULFO · *The Golden Cockerel & Other Writings*
translated by Douglas J. Weatherford · MEXICO

OLEG SENTSOV · *Life Went On Anyway*
translated by Uilleam Blacker · UKRAINE

MIKHAIL SHISHKIN · *Calligraphy Lesson: The Collected Stories*
translated by Marian Schwartz, Leo Shtutin, Mariya Bashkatova, Sylvia Maizell · RUSSIA

ÓFEIGUR SIGURÐSSON · *Öræfi: The Wasteland*
translated by Lytton Smith · ICELAND

MUSTAFA STITOU · *Two Half Faces*
translated by David Colmer · NETHERLANDS

FORTHCOMING FROM DEEP VELLUM

MIRCEA CĂRTĂRESCU · *Solenoid*
translated by Sean Cotter · ROMANIA

MATHILDE CLARK · *Lone Star*
translated by Martin Aitken · DENMARK

LOGEN CURE · *Welcome to Midland: Poems* · USA

CLAUDIA ULLOA DONOSO · *Little Bird,* translated by Lily Meyer · PERU/NORWAY

LEYLÂ ERBIL · *A Strange Woman*
translated by Nermin Menemencioğlu · TURKEY

FERNANDA GARCIA LAU · *Out of the Cage*
translated by Will Vanderhyden · ARGENTINA

ANNE GARRÉTA · *In/concrete*
translated by Emma Ramadan · FRANCE

JUNG YOUNG MOON · *Arriving in a Thick Fog*
translated by Mah Eunji and Jeffrey Karvonen · SOUTH KOREA

FISTON MWANZA MUJILA · *The Villain's Dance,* translated by Roland Glasser · *The River in the Belly: Selected Poems,* translated by Bret Maney · DEMOCRATIC REPUBLIC OF CONGO

LUDMILLA PETRUSHEVSKAYA · *Kidnapped: A Crime Story,* translated by Marian Schwartz · *The New Adventures of Helen: Magical Tales,* translated by Jane Bugaeva · RUSSIA

JULIE POOLE · *Bright Specimen: Poems from the Texas Herbarium* · USA

MANON STEFAN ROS · *The Blue Book of Nebo* · WALES

ETHAN RUTHERFORD · *Farthest South & Other Stories* · USA

BOB TRAMMELL · *The Origins of the Avant-Garde in Dallas & Other Stories* · USA